The Silent Voice

Books by Julia Cunningham

The Vision of François the Fox
Macaroon
Candle Tales
Dorp Dead
Dear Rat
Viollet
Onion Journey
Far in the Day
Burnish Me Bright
The Treasure Is the Rose
Maybe, a Mole
Come to the Edge
Tuppenny

THE SILENT VOICE
by Julia Cunningham

A Unicorn Book E. P. Dutton New York

Title page illustration by Ronald Himler

Library of Congress Cataloging in Publication Data

Cunningham, Julia.   The silent voice.
(A Unicorn book.)

Summary: A fourteen-year-old street urchin who cannot
speak is befriended by a famous Parisian mime. They
change each other's lives.

[1. Pantomime—Fiction.   2. Mutism—Fiction.
3. Orphans—Fiction.   4. Paris (France)—Fiction]   I. Title.
PZ7.C9167Si   1981   [Fic]   81-3091
ISBN 0-525-39295-5   AACR2

Published in the United States by E. P. Dutton, Inc.,
2 Park Avenue, New York, N.Y. 10016

Published simultaneously in Canada by Clarke,
Irwin & Company Limited, Toronto and Vancouver

Editor: Emilie McLeod   Designer: Riki Levinson

Printed in the U.S.A.
10 9 8 7 6 5 4 3 2

It is our wish, Auguste's and mine, that this, his final story, be shared with Emilie McLeod and those who have believed in him and have heard his voice in his silences.

~ 1 ~

The pavements were glazed with ice, the gutters filled, and beneath the shining lay stilled collections of trash Paris was frozen in winter.

The hour was early, the street empty of motion—almost. A huddled mound lay limp against a shuttered storefront, a bony hand protruding from its center. A passing wind fluttered the ragged sleeve, but the hand did not move.

Suddenly a girl whirled around the corner and skidded to a stop. *"Mon Dieu!"* she gasped. "Jerome, Francois, Thomas! Come here, quick! There's been a murder!"

Three boys clustered over the still form.

"Don't exaggerate, Astair," said the tallest, a boy so lean the front of his jacket seemed almost to meet its back.

"Oh, let her have her little dramas, Jerome," said the one called Thomas. He squatted on his haunches and poked his hand into the heap.

"Don't hurt him!" Astair's voice held command.

"Who could hurt a corpse?" Francois returned the girl's

1

order with some ferocity. He shoved at the body with his foot.

"You stop it, all of you!" Astair was standing very straight, her red hair blowing in the wind, her green eyes dark with anger.

"You want him?" mocked Francois. "You turning undertaker?"

The girl did not break her stance. She looked each of them in the eyes, first Francois, then Jerome, then the tiny Thomas, who walked on twisted legs. Gradually the group relaxed, silently reminded that she was their leader.

"What you want us to do?" said Jerome. He placed one hand on Astair's shoulder as if to reassure her that he was loyal to her.

"*Zut!*" exclaimed Thomas. "He's alive! Let's see what he's got on him. It's sure he's never going to need it."

Jerome pushed him away. "You're a fool, Thomas. He's got nothing. He's worse off than a beggar, even skinnier than me." Memory rose behind his words, a memory of himself running away from that last foster home walking so far, so hungry he had wanted to die. He wondered if this wanderer was just his height, maybe even his age. He glanced at the girl.

As if prompted, Astair spoke. "Take him to my room. It's better than the shed you people live in."

'But he's had it," protested Francois. "And if we're caught with a dead one they'll lock us up. They'll think it was our doing."

"But we can't just leave him," argued Thomas. "Not now we know he's alive."

"He won't be around long. I'll bet you on it," said Francois.

Jerome broke into the discussion. "But he's like us. Oh,

2

worse off, but the same. We've got to give him a chance."

"And if he dies?" But Francois's tone was less belligerent.

"Then we have another problem," said Astair firmly. "But right now he's going home with me."

Grumbling a little and with some roughness, the three boys lifted the unconscious boy by the arms and legs. Swinging him between them, they followed Astair the two blocks to a scarred, gray building with half its windows knocked out, where she had appropriated a room in the cellar.

"Put him on the mattress."

For a moment the four of them watched for some sign of vitality from the stretched-out figure. No breath filled the sunken cheeks and the blued skin of his hands did not respond to Astair's rubbing them between her own.

"He smells," commented Francois.

Thomas giggled. "And you, O lovely scent of Spring?"

Francois cuffed the smaller boy.

"Help me get his clothes off," said Astair. "He'll be warmer out of them. They are wet. And then you can go. I'll take care of him."

While she spoke she felt for the buttons of his ragged jacket, and suddenly her fingers closed around a hard object in a pouch underneath his shirt. She tugged at it, concealing the motion by pretending to have trouble undoing his coat. Something ripped. It must have been pinned on. She drew it out, covered by a corner of the jacket, which Jerome was now removing from the other side.

"Give me this," she said, taking the coat in her arms. "I'll see if I can mend it." She laid it in a cupboard on the near wall.

"Better mend him first," said Francois. He was rolling

3

off the boy's trousers. *'Mon Dieu!* Must have been starving for months! He's made of sticks!"

"Dirty, too," commented Jerome. "From a long time ago." His tone was distant, as though he were able to share the terrible days and nights of this stranger's journeyings.

"All right," said Astair briskly. "At least he'll warm up now." She had piled all three of her grimy blankets on top of him.

"And we'll be off," said Francois, "to entertain the first factory shift."

"We'll miss you," said Jerome, looking back at Astair as the three of them filed through the doorway.

Astair only waved, and as soon as they were out of sight she ran to get the crumpled jacket and extract the shape she had taken from the sick boy. Maybe she could sell whatever it was for enough to buy herself a new pair of shoes. The soles of her old ones had worn through and were stuffed with a layer of newspaper to keep out the wet.

The object was a small box made of red velvet. Astair hesitated, she didn't know why. She stroked the softness of it with a forefinger. Then, ridiculing her reluctance, she lifted the lid. Upon the black lining lay a medallion, a twelve-pointed circle of what she recognized to be gold, and at its center was a sapphire whose depths held a star.

For an instant her eyes shone bright. What a find! She stared at the boy who possessed such a treasure. Had he stolen it? How could he ever have gotten near anyone rich enough to own it? Curiosity guided her hand to his cheek and she pinched him lightly. She must have an answer.

Slowly his eyes opened. Something prompted Astair to close the box, something those eyes were telling her, beyond words, beyond thought. She placed it in one of his open hands and closed his fingers around it.

A shadow of a smile curved his mouth, and Astair's tongue became very busy. "We found you on the street nearly frozen, me and my comrades, and we brought you here to my place. Who are you? Where did you get that thing you had pinned to your shirt? You don't live in Paris or I would have seen you before."

Only silence met her questions.

"Are you too sick to talk? Try!" She wanted to shake him, the magic of the past moment now quite erased by her impatience.

Slowly he put one hand over his mouth, as though pushing back any words that might be filling it.

Astair gulped. "You're dumb, that's it! You can't talk!"

The boy nodded.

She turned away hurriedly. "But you must be starved. I've some soup left over from yesterday."

Astair talked steadily as she warmed the soup over a Sterno can and set out one cracked bowl and a spoon on the crate that was her table. She told the stranger how she and the three others managed to live by performing on street corners, by pilfering from markets, running errands, any way at all to keep their stomachs at least half-filled.

By the time the bowl was set in front of the boy, he was sitting on a stool before the crate, the blanket that had covered him wrapped his thinness.

"Don't worry about your clothes. I'll give them back just as soon as they dry, though they'd look better on a scarecrow. Might frighten the birds off for good."

The silent laughter that she saw on the boy's face brought her own laughter, enough for both of them.

When he had finished the soup, tipping the bowl to his

5

mouth to get the last drop, he pulled an imaginary pen from the air and began to write on paper that wasn't there.

Astair laughed again. "You're clever. Wait. I have a stub of chalk, and you can use the floor to write on. I can't—write, I mean. But I read a little."

She watched as he carefully rounded seven letters at her feet. *A-u-g-u-s-t-e*.

"But that must be your name!" she exclaimed.

He nodded, smiling.

"A kind of clown's name. Have you a second?"

He shook his head.

"Well, one's plenty. Auguste." She said it over to herself as if learning something important. Then, as she spread out his shirt and pants and jacket to dry over the window seat that was her bed, she continued. "I wish you could tell me where that medal came from. Oh, I know you can't and maybe you might not even want to. None of my business, really, in case you stole it. But don't let the gang see it. They'd turn it in for money."

She took a blanket from her bed and smoothed it over the lumpy floor mattress. "You'd better sleep, sleep a lot. I have to go to work now but I'll be back before dark and, with luck, bring something to eat that will have you dancing."

As she opened the door to leave, she glanced back at her new friend. She saw someone so frail, he was close to being no person at all. She was filled with tenderness and something beyond that. She sensed, she didn't know how, that in him was a power unlike anything she had ever touched.

2

Not until the next Sunday, six days later, was Auguste strong enough to accompany Astair and the boys into their world, the streets of Paris.

"You just take it slow," said Astair, "and watch what we do."

"Yes," said Thomas, hopping on one foot and whirling his short arms in the air. "Learn from your masters!"

Jerome pummeled him lightly on the back. "You'd be a good teacher for a stone statue."

The two of them laughed.

"Cut the comedy," said Francois, feeling somewhat left out. "We've another person to feed now."

Astair caught his criticism, but instead of reacting she rested her hands on Francois's shoulders and led him into a waltz, singing as they circled. The others sang with her, without words, and soon five passersby had paused to watch and listen.

Jerome nudged Thomas. "Get out your harmonica and put some life into it!"

Thomas obeyed. More people gathered, and when the dance ended, the cap he held out sagged with coins.

Astair had guided Auguste to the protection of a doorway, and although he was sheltered from the little jabs of wind that skittered around the corners, he couldn't seem to control his shivering.

It was Jerome who noticed his efforts to still the shivers. Jerome's lean face for the first time became friendly toward Astair's stray. "Come in with us. Don't be shy. Even if you can't sing maybe you can dance. At least that will warm you up, and if you're awkward they'll just think you're being funny." He held out his hand.

Auguste took it. Jerome winced, saying, "And I thought I was cold!"

He pulled the stranger into the open. "Francois, you show Auguste how to do a jig, a simple one, while Thomas provides the tune."

Francois, who was the same height as Auguste, put his left arm around Auguste's waist and showed him a pattern of toe-and-heel steps, first with one foot, then the other. Auguste imitated him without hesitation, without error. Separating himself, Francois went into a more complicated series, now twirling his body as he moved.

Astair was about to protest the intricacy of this first lesson when instantly she stopped short and watched.

Auguste had not only mastered Francois's direction but was improving on it. He moved—quick, free and so joyously that onlookers burst into spontaneous applause. Thomas quickened the harmonica's tempo to match the dance.

Then, just before the refrain's ending, Auguste wavered, his chest heaving into a cough. Both Jerome and Francois caught him under the arms.

"We'd best take him back," said Jerome. "He's had a bit too much for the first day out. You go on with it," he said to Astair. "We'll take care of him."

The two boys supported him to Astair's room and saw that he was comfortably tucked into the blankets on the window seat.

"We've got to return to work," said Jerome, "but you were great."

"Yes," agreed Francois. "When you get really healthy we'll earn enough to buy a new suit apiece and a diamond ring for Astair."

For the first time they saw Auguste smile, and he bowed to their compliments.

"Well, we'd better be going." Francois and Jerome left quickly, but just outside the door Auguste heard Jerome whistle and then say, "Where the devil do you suppose he learned all that?"

Auguste's smile did not diminish, but he fell into a day-dream so intense that two hours later he didn't hear the door open or notice the return of Astair.

She flopped on the seat beside the pensive boy. "Where were you just now?" she asked. "But I'm forgetting that you can't talk. It's very strange, you know, Auguste, but even before you went into the street with Francois I knew, somehow, that you would be better than him."

Then she laughed at herself and went to the rickety box that served as a cupboard. Digging into the pockets of her jacket, she drew out a can of beans, a small round of cheese and a half loaf of bread. She carefully stowed the beans on the shelf beside a sack of rice. "These are for when we haven't anything at all," she explained. "And that happens pretty often. But we'll have the cheese and bread between us. The boys are roasting potatoes."

9

She saw Auguste's question. "No. I'd rather eat with you. Besides, you're my responsibility."

She laid the meal on the crate and seated herself on the stool. She broke off an end piece of bread and stuffed half of it in her mouth, gesturing to Auguste to help himself. When she had satisfied her hunger, at least partially, she spoke again. "I'm not always with them, you know. I have my own concerns and interests." She saw that Auguste was listening intently. "For instance, I work for a lady who lives just down the block in that three-story building that has *School* written on its front." She chewed through a hunk of cheese, careful to see that Auguste had his share. "I'm sort of a messenger, more like an errand runner. But Madame Louva—she's the housekeeper there— she's got too much work to do and sometimes, maybe twice a week, she gives me a few francs for fetching and carrying. You'd like her. She's sort of severe and doesn't think too much of my living the way I do, but I think maybe she likes me, too. Never said so, just a feeling I have, like the feeling that you're more worthwhile than just anybody."

Having finished what food there was, she leaned her elbows on the crate. "Want me to tell you some more about myself?"

The boy nodded with evident eagerness.

Astair laughed. "I can't remember anyone wanting me to before." She sobered. "Sometimes, not often, but once in a while Madame Louva asks me into her kitchen. I keep quiet and just look and listen. And pretend," she added.

Auguste touched her arm lightly as if to encourage her to continue.

"Oh, it may sound stupid to you, but I pretend that I

live there." She looked down at her hands almost shyly and then she spoke more rapidly, as if to cover over what she had told him. "I don't really know what kind of a school it is where she works. I've seen the head of it, Monsieur Bernard. Once I followed him outdoors because I'd noticed that he went at least once a day and sometimes at night to another building not far from here. It's a theatre. Do you know what that is?"

Auguste's face was changing, as though a light behind his eyes had been turned up, brighter and brighter. Astair didn't need an answer.

"Then you do know. I sneaked in behind Monsieur Bernard—the man at the door wasn't on guard—and I'll never forget what I saw." Now her eyes were almost as glowing as the boy's, and her voice had dropped to a near whisper. "It was a big house full of hundreds of seats and in front was a kind of enormous room all lighted around the edges, and in this room were fake trees and a painted mountain in the back and then people in funny clothes talking at each other like real life, only it wasn't. And they came in and out and sometimes a man standing below stopped them and told them what to do."

She fell silent and seemed to forget her listener, lost in what she was remembering.

Then she saw that Auguste had freed himself of the blankets and was standing before her. He gestured toward the door, drew on an imaginary coat, and began to walk in place as though down a street. With a wide motion of his arms, he stopped. His face was lighted with wonder at something he pretended to see.

"You want me to take you there, is that what you are saying?" she asked.

11

Auguste nodded violently.

"Then I will. Tomorrow. I promise. But now I need to sleep. You, too. Good night, Auguste, and thank you."

Astair didn't know why she thanked this odd boy, but she was too tired to think about it. Curling up on her bench, she closed her eyes on all of it.

The boy lay quiet on his mattress, gazing for a long time into the darkness of the room.

⌁ 3 ⌁

It was late afternoon the next day before Astair could keep her promise. Thomas had been forced to stay off the streets by a severe chill, so the girl became the group's musician. Her instrument was simply a cracked recorder but it was better than nothing. Auguste had joined the others and contributed a brief pantomime of a bear chasing an elephant that brought in enough coins to buy Thomas a half liter of wine to cheer his supper.

Finally Astair, holding Auguste by the hand as though he were a child, led him to the back of the theatre.

"This is where I went in." She turned the doorknob very slowly to avoid any squeaking and peered in, then closed the door as cautiously. "The guard is there tonight. We can't get in." She guided Auguste around the block to the front entrance. "Now you've seen the whole building. All except the best," she added. "Maybe some other time we'll have better luck. Come on. My toes are frozen, they may drop off when I remove my shoes."

She laughed and skipped to the corner, but when she

13

looked back she saw that Auguste was standing, seemingly enchanted, gazing up at the billboards announcing something she couldn't read.

She whistled twice but he only glanced at her and then returned to studying the large, printed letters. She shrugged and left him to himself.

She could never know why the name, Le Théâtre Maritain, had sent the boy's mind shuttling backwards to a far ago memory. The same name was printed on a yellowed, forgotten theatre program, shown to him by the only person he had ever been given the chance to love. Nor could she know that this was the end of his quest. Auguste focused on one, sole desire. He must enter this place. Now. The memories could come later.

He raced to the back entry and without caution or caring let himself in, forgetting the threat of the guard. He stood watching the workers, who were intent on setting up the scenery. He had forgotten the cold of the world outside as he became absorbed in the crisscrossing of the people in front of him, each one moving purposefully, stirring the musty air as they passed him. He might have been a shadow pressed against the scarred wall.

Ahead of him on the lighted stage three boys who seemed about his age were grouped around a tall, graybearded man who was demonstrating to them a series of movements, aggressive advances and retreats.

"But Monsieur Bernard," said the one with the widest shoulders and curling, yellow hair, "that's just what I was doing."

"No, Philippe, you were not. You were dancing the action, not acting," the teacher replied. "Let's try it again, more forcefully."

Unaware that he had left the protection of the wall, Auguste moved up to the inner edge of the open curtain, half concealed by its thick folds. As he watched the mime, he felt the fatigue leave his body and he memorized the boy's movements.

"No," sighed Monsieur Bernard. "It's still not what I want. Take it from where your squires arrive. Jean-Louis, Raymond, you are in distress. Show it."

Something—the long line of the director's jaw, the delicate hollows at his temples, or was it the faint lines of sorrow around his mouth? Something thrust Auguste back to another time and an aching sadness.

He saw himself, Auguste, unwanted, orphaned, in the presence of the old man who had once been the greatest mime in France. He saw Hercule Hilaire, who had loved him, taught him, then left him in death. He recognized that this new teacher and Monsieur Hilaire shared the same gift. Auguste wished urgently to touch the transposed image of his dead master, to know the man was real. He took two steps forward.

Sudden pain gripped him. Someone who smelled of cigars loomed before him. He tried to twist free of the fingers that squeezed his shoulder muscles. Then a hoarse voice filled his ears.

"How did you get in here, you dirty little street rat? Came to steal, did you? Well, I'll soon rid the place of you!"

He shook Auguste violently, then pushed him to the floor.

The man had raised one foot to kick him when the other one called out, "Stop that, Bragge! Enough!"

Glancing up at Monsieur Bernard, Auguste impulsively reached out his hand and laid his forefinger on the felt toe of the man's shoe. Then he got to his feet. He waited.

"Want me to throw him out?" said the boy he now recognized as the one named Philippe. Two others were grinning behind him.

"Let him speak for himself," Monsieur Bernard said. "He may have business here in the theatre."

Philippe started to guffaw but was immediately silenced by the severity of his teacher's glance. "Not likely," the boy muttered.

Now the cigar smoker joined in. "My God, Bernard, you'd have every stray in Paris adopted and dressed like a lord if you had your way. That's your trouble. You're soft."

"That is as may be," said the master mime, his gaze steady on the boy in front of him. "You give the child no chance to answer. Come, don't be afraid. Tell us who you are and what you are doing here."

Auguste felt wonder at the closeness as he and Monsieur Bernard stood together in a kind of private silence. Philippe jeered, "Maybe his brains are missing," but it did not jar the communication between them.

Then Monsieur Bernard turned to Bragge and the three boys. He said, very slowly, as though he were himself surprised to know it, "The boy can't talk. He is a mute."

"So what?" said Bragge. "I'm the manager of a theatre, not a philanthropist, and he's cluttered up my stage." He shoved Auguste roughly. "You know where you came in. Now take the same way out!"

"No, wait." It was Monsieur Bernard. "I want to talk to the boy after rehearsal. Then he can go."

Bragge shrugged. "As you please. Just so he doesn't get into the dressing rooms or the offices. I'll hold you responsible."

Behind Monsieur Bernard's back Jean-Louis, stout, and blunt-featured in contrast to Raymond, who was slender, waggled his protruding tongue at Auguste. Raymond imitated his companion. Philippe showed his dislike for the intruder by a grimace of scorn.

Monsieur Bernard clapped his hands together and called out, "Places, please. We've work to do."

Auguste seated himself on the floor, once more in the shelter of the curtain. This had been the world of his beloved master. Hercule Hilaire had known this very stage. He shut his eyes for a moment and behind his lids formed the arch above him. The deep red curtain was closed now, the footlights restoring a rich luster to the folds of worn velvet. Alone before the curtain, facing the filled theatre, the gilt-edged boxes, the balcony that almost nudged the ceiling where painted cherubim circled the great crystal chandelier, stood his dead master, bowing his acknowledgment of unending applause.

Auguste was so locked into his vision he got up and moved backwards into the left wing, ready to embrace the reality of this beloved ghost. He collided with someone.

"That's enough!" growled the voice of Monsieur Bragge, the manager. "Out you go!"

He slapped the side of the boy's head as he reached the backstage door and flung him down the short flight of steps that touched the street. "And that's just a warning! Come back and I'll have your hide!" The door slammed on the light and the warmth within.

As Auguste walked slowly back to Astair's room, unaware of the night wind that stalked him, the threats were forgotten. Only the theatre lived in his mind, and the image of the teacher.

᪑ 4 ᪑

The next morning he woke early. For the first time since coming to Paris, he began the routine of exercises given him long ago by the master mime, who had shown him how his body could speak for him, be his voice.

When Astair opened her eyes her dingy room was filled with motion so graceful even the grayed light from the window seemed bright.

She waited until Auguste had finished, then got up and went to her cupboard. "That deserves a can of spaghetti," she said. "Been saving it for something special." She looked at her guest intently. "There was a moment just now when I wondered if you were real or if I had made you up. But I don't have enough imagination for that, not nearly."

Auguste stood smiling at her as she punctured the top of the can, poured the contents into a saucepan, and set it over the Sterno. When it was bubbling she scooped it all out onto a single dish. "We'll have to share. My butler smashed the others just last week and I had to fire him."

She handed the boy a battered spoon and the two of them soon scraped the plate clean.

Astair licked the smudges of tomato from the corners of her mouth and put on her jacket that was so much too big for her it looked like sacking. "Told the boys we'd meet them at the bird market. Come on."

She went out and Auguste hurried after her.

"Funny thing about that market," she chatted as they strode through a network of streets toward the river. "The people who stop to watch the birds seem gentler than most, maybe because they want something to love, something small and soft. You'll see."

The market announced itself before it came in sight. A cloud of chittering and cheeping and warbling hung over the block of cages and crates, and when Astair led him into the center of it, Auguste opened his own mouth as if he were compelled to sing with them, even silently.

At that instant they were surrounded.

"*Bonjour, Comtesse*," said Jerome.

"How goes it?" asked Francois. "Ready to serenade the money spenders?"

"Hope you don't mean the birds," said Thomas, hopping like a canary to keep warm.

"Not unless birdseed has suddenly turned into gold," countered Francois.

"What shall we give them?" asked Astair.

For reply Thomas drew out his harmonica and began a flurry of staccato notes that seemed to mock the birds. Francois picked up the cue and, bowing to the one person near them, leaped into a tap dance to match the rhythm of Thomas's notes. Six onlookers paused on their way to work, then eight more. When the act was over the group

19

had collected enough coins to buy breakfast at a cheap café. The coffee was left over from the night before, but it was hot.

Jerome sat back in his chair, his eyes grave. "Listen, friends, I've something to say. It's about him," and he nodded at Auguste.

"It's all very well to be charitable, to help others, all that Sunday stuff they tell you about over there." He jerked his thumb toward the cathedral on the south side of the square. "But I don't believe in getting thin while another gets fat."

Immediately interpreting his meaning, everyone looked at Auguste.

"Just a minute!" Astair's protest was vehement. "He did all right yesterday with the jig!"

"That's true," said Jerome, "but he couldn't finish. Nobody wants to see someone faint before their eyes. Too depressing. Keeps their hands out of their wallets."

Astair seemed to recognize the truth of what Jerome was saying, and she took a moment to search for a solution. Auguste mustn't be thrown out into the streets again. He wouldn't survive. But of what use was he to anyone? Unless—

"Give him a second chance. Come on—be fair. Francois?"

Francois nodded. "Just one more."

"Thomas?"

He also consented.

"Jerome?"

Jerome stared directly at Auguste. "You think you can make it?"

In answer Auguste got up and stood in the doorway. He waited.

"All right," said Jerome. "Let's see you prove it."

At Astair's suggestion they took the corner to the right of the cathedral. From long experience they knew that there would soon be an exodus from the morning mass.

"Need some music?" asked Thomas, wanting to help. He knew how he would feel if he were thrust out of the group.

Auguste shook his head.

"Just making it harder for yourself," advised Francois. "They like tunes."

Auguste did not respond. He gestured them back and then, as if inscribing a circle around himself with one turn, his arms outstretched, he performed what he had seen in the theatre, what the boy Philippe had failed to do. He mimed exactly what Monsieur Bernard had asked for. From a crouch close to the ground, defeat demonstrated in every line of his body, he gradually, inch by inch, began to rise from the cobblestones, and as he rose his movements quickened, his arms seemed to become wings, his head lifted as if to search the sky for passage. And then he leaped, once, twice, and a third time. Those who watched held their breaths. He was going to fly!

Auguste vanished into the crowd that had gathered.

There was silence, then applause. A man called out, "Come back!"

"Where did he go?"

"Who is he?"

Thomas had already taken off his cap to circulate it among the clapping people. The contributions were so heavy he had to hold on to the cap with both hands.

Astair hugged Jerome, who hugged Francois, who was shouting "Bravo!"

But Auguste was gone.

At last the audience gave up and went about their own affairs.

Jerome was about to start a search when they were approached by a very tall, aristocratic man in a cape. "Tell your friend that I must speak to him," he said.

Astair gasped. "But I know you. You're Monsieur Bernard and your housekeeper is Madame Louva and I work for her sometimes and you run that school and last night I took Auguste to your theatre."

The gentleman smiled and touched his forefinger to his mouth. "Hush, child. All that may be true and I'll not say it is uninteresting but I must talk to that boy, the one who flew into the clouds."

"You're going to make trouble for him, that it?" asked Jerome, now so relieved at Auguste's success he was ready to defend him right to the gate of any prison.

"Trouble?" The man frowned. "Is that what you imagine? Good Lord, no! I want him in my school!"

"But he hasn't any money," said Astair.

"Oh? Well, I wasn't thinking of money, though poor Madame Louva would have to stretch her budget if I gave her another mouth to feed."

"Oh, no, sir! Not really!" Astair flushed with a sudden solution. "You see, I do things for Madame Louva, and if you'd take Auguste into your school I'd give up doing errands for her and let him do them instead."

"I'm becoming a bit confused," said Monsieur Bernard, "but I'm certain my housekeeper will work something out. She always does. But what are we standing about for? Get that boy for me."

Before any of them could so much as turn to look around, Auguste appeared.

"Where were you?" demanded Jerome.

Monsieur Bernard made a gesture, brushing aside the question. Then he placed his hand on Auguste's shoulder. "I want you to come to my house at precisely eleven to-night. I will be back from the theatre by then and waiting. Knock softly. The rest of the household will be asleep. I will let you in and show you to your room. In the morning you will make the acquaintance of Madame Louva and the others. Agreed?"

Auguste blinked very rapidly as he nodded his head. His throat was tight with tears.

Monsieur Bernard reached into his pocket and drew out a large bill. He handed it to Astair. "This will buy all of you a good dinner, though I will be scolded for my generosity." He shook hands with each of them, and when he came to Auguste he smiled and said, "Thank you, my child, for your performance. We'll talk later."

Their dinner that evening was a feast with wine to complement the roast chicken, the fried potatoes, the salad and cheese and, last, two pastries apiece. But underneath their gaiety was a layer of sadness that Astair expressed for them all. "We'll miss you," she said. "We'll miss you a lot."

So when the last of the food was eaten they trooped out of the café-restaurant, separating with many reassurances to Auguste that they would see him again soon.

But Astair wasn't so sure. As she left him at the front door of the Ecole Bernard she felt lonely. She wanted to kiss him on both cheeks to show how she felt, but there was distance between them now, as though he had already gone down a road she couldn't travel. So it was with a handshake and a *"Bonsoir"* that they said good-bye. Then Auguste knocked at the door of Ecole Bernard. The door opened and he stepped through it and away.

↶ 5 ↷

When he awoke he was afraid to open his eyes, to leave the shelter of sleep. The night before, Monsieur Bernard had merely guided him into a dim room and left with a "good night." Now Auguste forced himself to look.

First he saw the round window. The frame was lined with the white of new snow, and beyond the glass was a horizon of rooftops, their chimneys plumed with spirals of smoke against a dove-gray sky. Then he saw the room. Crossbeams rose into the peak of the ceiling. It was an attic. He sniffed. The fragrance must be the smell of wood. In a far corner were stacked short logs and kindling. Three huge black trunks blotted out the opposite window. Beside the cot he was lying on, there was a stool and a small, rickety table. A chest lay at the foot of the cot.

He listened for sounds from the lower floors of the house, for clues that would ease this aloneness that encased him. But only the cry of a passing gull responded. He knew he must move toward whatever awaited him.

He sat up, threw back the blankets, and was just about to rise when the door flew open and in came a boy he had seen the night before, the fragile, weaker one. He was carrying a pair of shoes in his right hand.

"I'm Raymond. Madame Louva sent me up with these," he said in a voice thready with apprehension. He threw them onto the floor beside Auguste's cot, as if to avoid coming any closer. "She collected yours this morning. You were still asleep. They're not new, she said to tell you, but yours were only fit for the dustbin. Same size."

Auguste was now sitting on the edge of the bed. He groped for the shoes.

Raymond retreated still further. "You can't talk, can you?" he ventured.

Auguste shook his head. He leaned over to tie the laces of this sound, sturdy pair.

Raymond spoke again. "You crazy besides?"

Auguste looked upward at Raymond and his face changed, went vacant and slack. Raymond fled.

Auguste's expression righted itself into a smile but erased itself as he respread the blankets on the cot and then started very slowly down the stairs.

He hesitated on the last step, holding on to the banister as tightly as someone who was afraid of falling.

"Well, come in," said a voice from inside a lighted doorway. "It's plain enough this is the kitchen. Your nose should lead you to it."

The scent of coffee evoked such hunger in Auguste his stomach cramped. He had been too exhilarated the night before to enjoy the feast provided by Monsieur Bernard. He entered the large, square room lined with cupboards and counters, a round oak table encircled by six chairs at

25

its center. By the high black stove stood a woman who would have seemed tall if she had not been so plump. Her mouth was unsmiling, but her eyes were not unfriendly. "You need feeding. You were lucky yesterday. Monsieur Bernard told me about how he met you." She looked the boy over, an almost caring kind of inspection. "Sit down." She half filled a bowl with coffee, adding milk to the brim, then dropped in three lumps of sugar. "Yesterday's bread," she commented, slicing two thick pieces from the *baguette* under her arm, "but you can soak it in the coffee. Both of us are earlier than the baker this morning."

Auguste took the bowl and bread from her hands but did not seat himself. He gulped down the fragrant liquid and then finished the bread.

"I am Madame Louva," she began as she sat down at the table, "Monsieur Bernard's housekeeper and fortunate indeed to be so."

She crossed her arms and leaned them on the table. "You must be asking yourself many questions. Let me tell you about us. There's Monsieur Bernard and me, of course. Then the three boarders, Philippe, Jean-Louis and Raymond. Their parents pay us well to keep them here or I wouldn't consent to it. They are not quality, in my manner of thinking. Oh, they've been taught their manners like all rich children, but the ways of their hearts are a different matter. Yes, we are a school here. The École Bernard. The master, I am told and I've no doubts as to the truth of it, is the greatest mime in this country, though"—she sighed—"he's aging now." She looked into a distance Auguste could not share. "It's difficult for him. I know it. He knows it. But we never mention such things. There is much for him yet to do as a teacher."

Her gaze returned to the boy opposite her. "But perhaps I seem to you to be talking nonsense. What can you, a child with no family name, no home, no certain memories, comprehend? Surely not even what a true mime is." Her eyes spoke her sympathy.

Auguste, who had been completely absorbed in the warmth and presence of this woman who had so plainly made him welcome, suddenly tensed at her last words. He involuntarily touched his left side, felt under the wool of his worn shirt to see if his secret was safe. His fingers reassured him that the little box within its leather pouch was still there, refastened securely by Astair with a safety pin.

"Do you feel ill, child?" Madame Louva could not interpret this gesture.

He smiled and shook his head.

"But you do not speak. Why? Am I so fearsome?"

Auguste placed one hand over his mouth, the other to his throat.

"Monsieur Bernard neglected to tell me!" The housekeeper murmured something under her breath, not allowing her sympathy to become words. She spoke quickly. "But certainly we must know your name. To be nameless in the world is to be lost. Can you write?"

Auguste nodded.

"Then get my shopping pad from the ledge by the window. You'll find a pencil beside it. Introduce yourself."

Auguste obeyed and handed her the slip of paper, upon which he had written *Auguste*.

Madame Louva smiled now for the first time. "An honorable name, but like you it needs filling out. What follows?"

For answer Auguste simply took the scrap from her and crumpled it into a ball.

"Oh, one of those," she said as to herself. "Roadside children we used to call them in my village." She got to her feet and, going to the boy, pulled out a chair. "Sit here, Auguste," she said and then returned to the stove, where she poured him a second bowl. She laid the remaining length of bread and a knife in front of him. "Take as much as you wish. The others won't be down for a little while."

At that moment, as if to contradict her, Raymond entered with Jean-Louis. They scraped into tneir chairs and then sat back to be served. Jean-Louis looked condescendingly at Auguste. "The dummy still here? Thought you would have put him out by now."

Madame Louva set their breakfast before them, not regretting the day-old bread, adding a pot of plum preserves. "Who is here and who is not is the business of those who run this school, not yours," she said firmly. "Where is Philippe?"

"He decided to eat in his room," said Raymond. "I'll take it up to him."

With a semblance of patience she did not feel, the housekeeper began to set a tray. Monsieur Bernard's accounts were precarious and needed the added income that came from the boarders.

"Dummy got a name?" asked Jean-Louis.

"Idiot, maybe," said Raymond and the two of them laughed.

"Eat, messieurs," said Madame Louva, "or you'll be late for the morning practice."

Jean-Louis dabbled the crust of his bread idly in his coffee and stared at Auguste. "I don't know if I wish to be at the same table with a social inferior."

Raymond giggled. "Fancy phrase for so early in the day."

The housekeeper set down the milk pitcher so hard the tray clanged. "I say who sits where and when and our guest is to be allowed to finish his breakfast in peace."

Jean-Louis snickered.

At that moment Philippe strode into the kitchen. "Got tired of waiting," he announced. All three boarders looked toward Auguste. "My place taken?" asked Philippe, his stance expressing insolence.

Auguste slid out of his chair and went to where Madame Louva was standing before the refrigerator, Philippe's tray held a little high, as though she were prepared to slam it to the floor. Her mouth tightened against wording her anger as she set it in front of him. She turned from the boys.

Auguste returned her look with such a smile, wry at the corners, that she could only smile too. She was filled with a surprising rise of longing for this tall weed of a boy before her, destined to one day die in an alley and no one to sorrow over his absence. She suddenly wanted to belong to him. Not he to her but she to him. She guessed him to be fifteen and here she was, nearly an old woman, wishing she were at least a distant cousin.

It was Auguste who broke the moment. He started across the threshold and then stepped back to permit Monsieur Bernard to enter.

The older man tapped his arm. "Feeling fit?" The lines around his mouth deepened as he smiled. He waved to the others. "*Bonjour, mes élèves* How goes it this morning?"

The three responded briefly and began a conversation among themselves in undertones.

"Well, do you want to keep him?" Monsieur Bernard asked his housekeeper. "I decide nothing without your approval."

The three boys cut off their chatter abruptly.

All she replied was, "Yes, monsieur, I do."

Monsieur Bernard rubbed his eyes tiredly. He now addressed Auguste. "We could use a general help here to run errands for Madame Louva, do the cleaning. I can't pay you, you understand that. It would be work in exchange for room and board and lessons. If that satisfies you, you may stay."

Auguste nodded, smiling widely.

Madame Louva was now busily assembling her patron's meal.

Monsieur Bernard dismissed it with a gesture. "Just coffee, please. I slept poorly."

She gave him what he asked for and he drank half of it. Then, pointing at Auguste, he left the table saying, "I'll expect you in the studio in five minutes."

He was no sooner gone than Philippe spoke up. "You keep out of my way, hear me, or I'll black both of those wide eyes for you."

At the sink, washing the dishes, Madame Louva refrained from interference. The boy would have to learn for himself how to adjust to her household. If he did, he would be useful. If not, he would have to go.

Auguste showed no reaction to Philippe's taunt and slowly ascended the stairway after the master.

∾ 6 ∾

The instant Auguste entered the studio he knew he belonged there. The wall of mirrors with the dance bar along their length, the ceiling-high windows opposite, the rubbed surface of the unpolished floor, all seemed familiar. He might have dreamed them so often they had become reality.

He didn't know that his face was open with delight.

"Like it, do you?" said Monsieur Bernard, slightly startled by this boy's unusual pleasure.

Auguste nodded vehemently.

"Well, it may be old, needing paint and an assiduous window cleaner, but there's space here for invention of any kind." He strode the length of the room and back. "Space to stretch the mind. But you'll believe I always talk nonsense. To work. You'll find a broom in the attic and Madame Louva will give you water, soap and rags. Start with the mirrors. Be pleasant to see the clouds again."

He now began a series of exercises, bending from the waist to the right and left and, last, forward. He seemed to have forgotten the boy.

31

Auguste watched him for a moment, sadness drawing his face even thinner. He was remembering his dead master instructing him in these same motions. Auguste's body involuntarily contracted into that held stillness that preceded movement.

Then swiftly he pivoted on his heel and took the stairs two at a time up to the attic. First he drew the broom from the one closet and leaned it against the doorjamb, almost ready but not just yet. Sitting down on the stool, he carefully unfastened the little pouch from under his shirt and slipped it out. From this he lifted the red velvet box. He looked for a second through the window, not seeing what was there, but into the past.

His mind returned to the evening Monsieur Hilaire, so soon to die, had said to him, "I have no substance to leave you, no treasure but this." Auguste now opened the box. There lay the medallion. Auguste touched its shining with his fingertips, then heard again the words of his master.

"At my farewell performance, before the footlights were extinguished and the stage cooled, I was presented with this last honor. I give it to you now before you have earned it because I will not be there to applaud your triumph. Hide it, my child, hide it in safety, and when you arrive at the moment to accept it—and you will know when that moment comes, I promise you—listen to the silence and remember me."

The boy touched it to his cheek and then slowly returned it to the box, the pouch, and finally secured it again under his shirt.

Now carrying the broom, he hurried down the three flights to the kitchen. The boarders were gone. Madame Louva greeted him with "Acquainted with the studio now, are you? Well, that's the most important room in the school so see that you keep it properly." She heard the strictness in her own voice but did not restrain it. She was a little ashamed of her former softness toward this poor unfortunate boy off the streets. God knew the alleys were full of others just like him. She didn't understand that pe culiar instant, when something had caused her to believe this one was different.

"Soap's already in the bucket under the sink," she continued. "Mirrors and windows today. You'll find a short ladder in the closet. And no streaks or you'll do them again." Her severity relented a notch as she looked into the deep attentiveness of his eyes. "Show you're willing and I'll treat you right. You do understand everything I say, don't you?"

Auguste's nod was quick as a bird's.

"Look bright enough, at that."

Auguste gestured the wringing out of an invisible rag.

Madame Louva laughed. "Better than talk, I'd say. Here, *mon petit*." She drew out a large cloth that had been hung to dry at the side of the stove and, stooping in spite of the twinge in her back, she handed him the filled bucket at the same time.

Feeling more comfortable with herself, she began to hum as she started to peel the potatoes for lunch.

Auguste offered a smile as his thanks, though she did not see it. He hurried to the studio.

Alone, he scanned the long, light room down each wall. He imagined himself in the center, feeling the length and height of it as if the dimensions were measured in a radius from his body. Now he knew the studio.

Lifting the ladder from the closet, his pail arranged below, he climbed to the top rung and began to wet down the first section of mirror. Washing and drying in long sweeps, he soon finished half the wall of glass and had moved to the next half when the first students, six boys and three girls, poured in, laughing and talking. They ignored the boy on the ladder.

Three more entered, then Philippe and the other boarders. They, too, paid no attention to the rapid actions of the worker.

With one last strip of glass to finish, Auguste felt a tap on his back. It was Monsieur Bernard. "Time enough after the class is terminated," he said. "We'll need the bar, so why not tackle the windows?"

The teacher clapped his hands together twice and the fifteen pupils immediately formed a line.

"First, breathing, then walking, heel, toe and reverse, then running. You know the routine." At the signal of another clap, the class began to obey the instructions in almost perfect unison.

Auguste turned his head to watch as he mopped at the window squares. These were the same exercises Monsieur Hilaire had taught him, but here the great mirrors disclosed mistakes as certainly as they imagined excellence. The routines at the bar were unfamiliar to him, and he recorded them in his head until the day when Monsieur Bernard would coach him.

Two hours later the insides of the panes glistened. The last exercise, all the students running in a circle, had just been called by Monsieur Bernard.

Auguste gazed out at the street below. Ranked side by side were the bakery, the grocery, the meat shop, the café, then a newspaper stand, a florist and a small restaurant, a church spire rising behind it. Here was a whole world in one tiny place, Auguste thought to himself, surrounded by hundreds of other neighborhood worlds, all bound together by the curves and angles of hundreds of paved streets. He wished for wings so that he might look down upon the whole of it and, flying higher, see it dwindle into a miniature he could carry back to his attic.

A blow on his back jolted him from his vision. The students were now in a quickstep. He couldn't know who had hit him. Once more he looked downward from the window. Three women were grouped before the bakery. A child was solemnly buying an apple from the proprietor of the fruit and vegetable stand outside the shop.

Then Auguste glimpsed Astair's flaring red hair. He watched her take advantage of the grocer's attention to the child. Quickly she thrust two pears into the pocket of her jacket and nonchalantly walked away.

Once more the blow on his back pulled him back into the room. The master was speaking. "That will be all for this morning. We will reassemble at the theatre after the lunch period. Class dismissed."

After the fifteen pupils followed Monsieur Bernard from the studio, Auguste put away the ladder and placed the bucket and rags by the door. He took up the broom for a partner and danced the circumference of the room. He ran and leaped and then slowed to a waltz. A bird peered in from the window ledge and sang, as though to provide music for this solitary dancer. Auguste stopped, bowed to the bird, and wheeled into the movements of flight, as though he were truly aloft in the wind above the vast pattern of Paris.

7

When Auguste had finished washing down the floor, he restored the broom to the attic and returned to the kitchen. He rinsed out the bucket, rehung the wet cloths by the stove and then stood by the table. He watched Madame Louva put a bulging sandwich, a pear and a square of frosted cake into a paper box. She took a length of used string from a shelf and tied it around the box, leaving a loop at the top for carrying.

"This is Monsieur Bernard's lunch. He sends the boarders back but most of the time forgets to come himself. His head is too full of everything else. So I want you to be sure he gets this. Do you know the way to the theatre?"

Auguste nodded.

She handed the box to him, giving him a keen look as though to assure herself of his reliability. What she saw pleased her, for she patted him once on the shoulder and then gave him a tiny push toward the door.

Auguste almost ran the blocks to the theatre, careful not to joggle the contents of the master's meal. The stage doorman let him pass when he saw the box, recognizing it to have come from Madame Louva.

The rehearsal was just ending and Auguste stationed himself inconspicuously in the wings. Philippe, waving an invisible whip, was leading the others in a ring, and Auguste realized that this was a circus parade with Philippe the ringmaster. More or less skillfully, the others had taken the parts of animals and performers: two horses, a bear, three elephants, two jugglers, a girl who may have been an aerialist, and four clowns. Calliope music from a record player backstage set the rhythm.

"I want more liveliness from the clowns. Be inventive!" called Monsieur Bernard from the empty theatre. "You've all been to circuses—remember what you saw! Start again, entering from stage right."

But the second time around was even less animated. "All right," said their teacher, "that's enough for now. We'll have to work harder if we are to be acceptable at the young count's birthday party Saturday. I won't present anything that is second-rate. Dismissed for lunch. Come back at three."

Auguste, who had become a clown in his head, suddenly felt the box lunch being snatched from his hands. It was Jean-Louis. "I'll deliver this," he said roughly. "What are you doing here anyway?"

"Yes, I'd like an answer to that myself," said the stage manager. "Thought you'd been disposed of long ago."

"No," interposed Monsieur Bernard. "He's working in the school for Madame Louva. She needed assistance."

"Well, just keep him out of the theatre. Don't like freaks anywhere near me, never did."

Monsieur Bernard thanked Jean-Louis and said to Au-

37

guste, "There'll be less trouble if you stay away from the theatre, child," and then gestured for him to go.

Auguste walked slowly back through the puddled streets. The snow had melted, leaving the gutters choked with gray slush. In the cracks between cobblestones floated bits of rubbish in blackened water. He drew his ragged collar up around his neck and blew into his cupped hands to warm his fingers.

A tirade of angry words flooded the morning. He lifted his head. The baker's wife leaned from her doorway, hands on her ample hips, yelling down at Astair, who was sitting on the stoop of the bakery, hugging herself against the cold.

"I'll have the police on you, you nasty little thief! Life's hard enough. God knows mine is no bunch of violets and you're not going to steal the bread my husband gets up to bake at two in the morning." She held a single roll in one hand. "I'd rather give it to the sewer than to a wicked bundle of trash like you!" She aimed the roll at the drain hole across the street. It fell in and vanished. "That'll teach you what you're worth. Wish I could throw you in after it!"

"And you would, if you could," said the girl defiantly. "I know your type. Wear a cross to mass on Sunday and beat your husband on Monday."

The woman bent forward, her arm outstretched to slap Astair, but the girl was too nimble for her and easily dodged the blow.

Auguste drew six imaginary balls from his jacket pockets and began to toss them into the winter air. His concentration was so complete, the illusion so real, the baker woman stopped still to watch, forgetting to close her

mouth. Astair looked on in a sudden shift from fierceness
to pleasure.

Five passersby paused to watch.

Auguste pretended to drop one of the flying balls. An
unconscious sigh came from the onlookers. He recovered
it and now added hoops to each arm and around his left
ankle. He kept all nine moving for a long moment. Then,
catching the balls in the bowl of his hands, he threw them
all up together and, tossing the invisible hoops after them,
bowed to the small audience that now numbered twenty.

They clapped and a scatter of change clicked onto the
pavement. With the swiftness of a cat, the girl scooped up
the coins and handed them to Auguste. The people dispersed.

"You had bells on your cap, didn't you?" she said, her
smile so broad it erased the hollowness of her cheeks. "I
saw them."

Auguste handed the money to the baker's wife and then
ushered his friend into the steamy fragrance of the shop.
He pointed to the glass case filled with pastries, then
glanced at the woman. She counted the coins and then
nodded. "Take your choice. But one only."

"You choose," said Astair. "You earned it."

Auguste simply stepped back.

"Then I will," she said and scanned the entire selection,
considering each one in turn. At last she picked out a high
oblong layered with custard, minced chestnuts and
whipped cream. The top was powdered with confec-
tioner's sugar. The baker woman handed it to her on a
piece of waxed paper.

"I'd rather eat it outside," Astair said, and they left the
bakery and sat together on the stoop.

"You see, I want to make it last," she explained. "Never had anything like this before." She nibbled at one side. "You get half."

Auguste shook his head.

"How's it going?" she asked. "They treat you right?"

Auguste rose and wielded a broom that had no effect on the damp sidewalk.

Astair laughed. "I used to do housework, too, but they let me go. Said I wasn't strong enough to push back the heavy furniture and carry their boxes. I think they must have been loaded with bricks. I couldn't budge them. That's when I went to live in my basement."

Auguste looked up at the sky between the rooftops. Rain hung above them in soot-colored clouds. He held out his hand in farewell.

"When will I see you again?" asked the girl. "Tell you what. I have a stub of chalk, see?" She took it out of her skirt pocket. "When I plan to be near, I'll make a little star on the side of the bakery, right here. That means we'll meet, if we can, in the Parc Molière just around the corner between four and six. Agreed?"

Auguste shrugged.

"But you'll try, won't you?"

He nodded emphatically and ran off in the direction of the school.

Astair looked after her friend, the still uneaten half of pastry carefully cupped in her hand, her face no longer pale. She strode off down the street with new vigor in her walk.

Auguste arrived at the front steps of the school just behind the housekeeper, who was burdened with two large market baskets. She put them down on the kitchen table with a relieved sigh. "Next time," she said to Auguste, "no loitering. I could have used you to help me manage this load. Have a dinner to get tonight. Monsieur Bragge and Madame Trollant, Philippe's mother, are coming and the master likes everything proper. You can begin by peeling the onions."

They worked together silently, Madame Louva occasionally glancing over at the boy, and it was not until she had finished slicing the green beans that she spoke again. "How old are you, child?"

Going to the counter where she kept her shopping tablet, he took up the pencil beside it and slowly inscribed a line of words. He handed it to the housekeeper.

She read it twice. "*Chère madame*, I am aged fourteen years. I am grateful for your kindness."

Madame Louva put down her paring knife and looked directly into his eyes. "Whoever and whatever you are, *mon petit*, you are a gentleman."

The boy felt suddenly shy and he broke the look between them.

"Oh, no need to be embarrassed by an old woman's opinion. I speak the truth as I see it and I miss very little. Have you any family?"

Auguste shook his head.

"A waif? Then how were you brought up?"

The boy got to his feet. He imitated in turn a chicken, a cow and a donkey, ending with the latter's tall ears and a silent bray.

Madame Louva laughed. "On a farm, surely."

Auguste bowed. Then, as though spreading straw in a nest about himself, he mimed sleep.

"And you slept in a barn."

41

The boy nodded.

"Whoever took you in couldn't have been very cordial. A barn's not the warmest winter palace."

Auguste now became clumsy, as though with stoutness. He stomped as he walked, head thrust forward.

The housekeeper chuckled. "I know the type. Peasant-minded, mean as a brood sow, brain of an ox. You ran away?"

Auguste's face suddenly lost its playfulness. He shuddered, remembering how the townspeople of that village had driven him out, believing him to be evil.

His pain was apparent to the housekeeper. "That's enough information for now," she said, rising from her chair. "Finish those onions and then you can ship the cream for me. Just one more thing. I'm going to offer you some advice. I don't know how long Monsieur Bernard will keep you, but for as long as he does you must be prudent in your dealings with Philippe. He is not a good person, and because you cannot protest he will act the bully. He does it to Raymond or anyone he considers weaker than himself. Keep out of his way as much as you can."

Auguste stiffened.

Madame Louva noted his reaction. "I can see that you have suffered, *mon petit*, but I also see that you are no stranger to courage. I shall trust you to use it."

~ 8 ~

That evening the three boarders were to have their supper in the kitchen. Madame Louva had made it plain that her first responsibility was to the guests in the dining room. This was an important evening. Not even Philippe was to be included.

Madame Trollant had arrived twenty minutes late. While she greeted Philippe, the housekeeper feared for the onion soup. After it was served and complimented, her nervousness diminished. When she had taken in the fish course she visibly relaxed. She turned to the four boys.

"Tonight it is family style. Help yourselves and keep the peace. Auguste, put the casserole on the table. The salad is over there with the cheese and fruit when you are ready for them."

The conversation of the three adults in the next room could be clearly heard in the kitchen.

Philippe's mother, her voice elegantly strident, dominated the conversation.

"I want a full accounting, Bernard, a *full* accounting.

Your school is not a charity, you know. That's not sensible. You do have a complete enrollment, have you not?"

"As many as I can effectively teach," was Monsieur Bernard's reply.

"And I assume they are all paying the required tuition?"

"Let it go for now," said Monsieur Bragge. "You're spoiling this delicious dinner."

"The taste of money never caused you an illness," came the tart response from Madame Trollant. "Well Bernard?"

"Three are on scholarship," said the master mime.

"I thought as much! And you expect me to make up the difference. Really, Bernard, you are a fool. I'm fond of you in my way, but that doesn't stop me from seeing you as you are, an impractical artist."

Auguste heard Madame Louva, who was slicing the beef roast, mutter almost inaudibly, "Better that than a woman with a heart of steel."

The theatre manager's voice boomed. "Now, now, we all know that Bernard is the finest in his field—"

"Was," interrupted Madame Trollant. "Let us not deceive ourselves—the company needs a new star."

"And you have found one, *chère collègue?*" Monsieur Bernard's tones remained sweet.

"But is it necessary to search?" was her reply.

"Meaning?" asked Bragge.

Now Monsieur Bernard's voice strengthened. "In my company, there is no star." He paused. "Not of the quality you have just said I was."

"Then you must make one."

"You speak of Philippe, do you not?" The teacher did not wait for her predictable answer but went on. "A premier mime, an artist of the first rank, shows himself long

44

before the years of learning are achieved. And candidly, dear lady, though Philippe is undoubtedly gifted, he has not yet evidenced this quality."

Madame Louva came back in the kitchen after serving the salad. She noticed that no one but Auguste was eating. The others were intent on the talk from the other room. She shut the kitchen door and the words beyond it could no longer be heard clearly, but there was no mistaking the rising anger in Madame Trollant's voice.

"Pay attention to your supper or you'll go to bed hungry" Madame Louva said crossly. "I've yet two courses to present and then the dishes to do. The good Lord knows how long Monsieur Bragge will linger over his brandy. So eat up."

Philippe began to pat his mashed potatoes into the shape of a moon-face that lacked a mouth.

"Guess who," he said to Jean-Louis and Raymond.

Raymond tittered and pointed to Auguste.

"Bright boy," commented Philippe. He nudged Auguste. "Think it's a good likeness?"

Auguste pretended not to understand.

Philippe smashed the face with the flat of his spoon. Then he drummed one foot against the table leg and winked at Jean-Louis. The meaning of the signal was obeyed, and Jean-Louis aimed a swift kick at Auguste's leg under the table. It contacted the boy's shinbone and Auguste gasped.

Madame Louva turned from the counter. "What's the trouble here?" she said. None of the faces betrayed what had happened. She had no sooner gone back to filling the dessert bowls with fruit than once more Philippe winked, this time toward Raymond as well.

45

Auguste did not wait for further bruising. He got up from the table, half of his dinner still on his plate.

He walked to the sink and began to fill the dishpan with hot water.

"Well," said Philippe, "look at our little scullery maid."

Madame Louva had had enough. Her beloved patron was undergoing an inquisition from Madame Trollant and only she knew how ill-equipped this dedicated man was to defend himself. No one seemed to be giving full appreciation to her dinner—how could they in such an atmosphere?—and now the boys were teasing Auguste.

"Not one more word!" she said explosively. "Not one! The first to speak will get out of my kitchen immediately!"

Subdued, the three boys hastily finished their supper and then went to their rooms. Only Auguste was left, and when he had washed and dried the last coffee cup he quietly walked from the house into the serenity of the night.

The boy did not smell the pungent musk of a woodsmoke that drifted down from the chimneys or taste the air that might have been frosted spring water. Even the stone step he chose to sit on, its chill penetrating the wool of his pants, did not exist for him. All the hoping he had done a few days ago, having found the school and been given a job to pay for food and shelter, was as ephemeral as the ashes of a burned twig. Even remembering the occasional kindness of Madame Louva could not color the bleakness. The image of the three boys at the supper table blanked her from his mind. They would assassinate any chance to learn that he might be given.

He suddenly became again the dirty, deserted child enslaved by a farm woman who intended to work him until he sickened. He wished for the isolation of the barn that had been his refuge from the beatings and the hunger. On the steps of this house in Paris he crouched into himself, his head down, his arms around his ears shutting off all sound but the beating of his heart, and willed himself to die.

A softness brushed his clenched hands, twice, three times, back and forth. A warm softness. Now it leaned against him, then passed between his legs. Slowly Auguste raised his head and looked directly into the green eyes of a black cat. They stared at one another for a moment and then Auguste reached out and took the animal into his hands, stroking its back as he lifted it to lie against his chest.

"Have you something to tell me?" he asked the cat silently, somehow certain that this messenger from the night would know his thought. The thrumming of its purr was answer enough and Auguste was pulled back to the present.

He stayed still and close to this live comforting warmth for a few moments, then got up. The cat did not stir. Auguste couldn't shovel him back into the night. Then he remembered the Parc Molière, the place Astair had chosen for them to meet.

Walking smoothly, gliding heel to toe, he covered the three blocks to the triangle of green, centered by a statue ringed by a row of plane trees. He lifted the cat into the lap of the statue but the animal speared Auguste's jacket with its claws and wouldn't let go. The purring had ceased.

Auguste began to circle one of the trees, slowly turning. The cat relaxed its claws, and very, very gently Auguste raised it into the lowest crotch of the tree. Then, before the cat could move, the boy resumed his dreamlike turns, as though he were weaving a web around the cat's perch. The cat watched, crouched low. Gradually Auguste widened the circle until he arrived at the sidewalk. He turned away and swiftly retraced his way back to the school. He entered the house, closing the front door behind him, and ran up to his room.

For a few minutes he sat on the edge of the cot, his body tensed against a thought he couldn't exorcise. He felt very small as he remembered lying on the straw of that far, long-ago barn, lost in the same silent aloneness into which he had been born.

Suddenly he stood up. He had to go to the window. He had to look down. There, as though summoned, was the cat sitting on the pavement, waiting.

Auguste did not hesitate. He went down to the second floor, then chose the back stairs that led into the basement. A moment later, without a creak, he pushed open the cellar door that exited onto the sidewalk, slipped to the front of the house and scooped up the cat.

He was about to mount the rear staircase again when he heard Monsieur Bernard, Bragge and Madame Trollant talking in the hall. He hid under the angle of the stairs. He would have to stay there until they left.

"It should be a fine day in the country. I've sent orders to the château that we are coming," Madame Trollant was saying. "I'll send the car for you tomorrow at eight sharp. Be sure Philippe and his friends are ready."

Auguste heard Madame Louva respond, "Certainly, madame."

"Monsieur Bernard"—it was Madame Louva again—"what about the new boy, Auguste?"

"He can fend for himself," interjected Madame Trollant, "of that I am sure. God knows he wouldn't fit in with our party."

Auguste heard Monsieur Bragge's loud belly laugh. "About as well as a stray cat!"

"I beg your pardon, madame," said the housekeeper, "but I was asking Monsieur Bernard."

"Oh, he'll be all right alone. Just see that he has enough to eat. We won't be back until late in the evening."

"Never fear about that, monsieur." Madame Louva's voice had a smile in it. "In that case, may I be permitted to spend the day with my sister in Louvennes? I haven't seen her since October."

"And not join us? We will miss you. But of course do as you wish, whatever gives you the most pleasure."

"Thank you, monsieur."

"Now," said Madame Trollant, "that all is so thoroughly arranged, I confess I am wilting with fatigue. Do help me with my coat, dear host. My chauffeur has been outside quite long enough while we gossip here in the hall."

The voices receded, and finally Auguste heard the housekeeper and her patron say good-night to the guests and to each other. The cat gave a tiny mew as they climbed the stairs but Madame Louva's heavy tread extinguished the sound.

Auguste tiptoed quickly up to the attic and released the cat, who began a slow, surveying inspection of the long room. He stood and watched his new friend, memorizing the grace of him.

❧ 9 ❧

The next morning when they had all gone, Madame Louva and Auguste conferred in the kitchen. "I've left quite enough food for you," she said. "In fact, enough for ten of you. You are too thin. Why not pretend you've invited yourself to a feast? Then you'll be sure to take what you wish and as much as you wish."

Auguste's smile was so bright it seemed to the housekeeper to be almost as though a slash of light had crossed his face.

"You're an odd one." She paused and then continued "I'm a sensible woman and no nonsense, always have been, and I'm going to tell you something that sounds a bit foolish. I feel as though I've known you for a very long time. Droll, isn't it?"

For reply Auguste lifted her coat from its hanger in the hall and held it for her to slip into. Then, with a bow, he held out her black silk Sunday hat.

Madame Louva laughed. "It's been a great while since a gentleman helped me into my coat." She put on the hat.

50

Then she reached in her handbag. "I almost forgot. Here is a spare key in case you go out, and I expect you will. I've set the lock to secure the door automatically."

Auguste rubbed the little piece of metal in his right hand. He had never been trusted with a key to anywhere.

She saw his pleasure. "Master of the house, that's what you are now. Well, I must be off or I'll miss the early bus. A good day to you, Monsieur Auguste!"

Auguste made her a reverence, sweeping the floor with an imaginary plumed hat.

Once alone, he cleaned the studio. He did an hour of exercises, combining the ones his old master, Hilaire, had taught him with those of the École Bernard. Then he returned to the kitchen. After he scrubbed the floor, he opened the refrigerator. Cheese, eggs, and butter filled the top shelf. He saw that the housekeeper had put out a basket of apples and left the lid of the potato bin tipped up, as though to invite him to take what he wanted.

For an instant he felt hollow with aloneness. Then an idea came to him. What if he invited Astair to join his feast?

Checking his pocket for the key, he ran from the house and across the street. The tiny, crooked star was chalked on the baker's sill. He raced to the park.

Strollers walked in the still meager sunlight. Dogs trotted beside them on leashes or chased each other, barking, in and out of the columns of trees. The benches and spindly iron chairs were occupied by men and women, some reading, some chatting to neighbors, some very old, their eyes seemingly fixed, unobserving, in a kind of dreaming. There was no sign of Astair.

Auguste sat on the edge of a large stone basin filled by

the water spilling down from a steeple of giant urns that centered the pool. He dabbled his fingers in its coolness. A horse and rider passed by in the *allée* between the chestnut trees. The horse was white. Auguste remembered he, too, had once ridden a white horse, and the memory was so potent he closed his eyes to savor it.

Something pushed him backward, and he had to grip the rim of the fountain to keep from tumbling into the water. It was Astair.

"I hoped you would come," she said through her laughter. "What shall we do today? I tell you," she chattered on, not pausing for Auguste to respond, "let's pretend we are very rich, all in our best clothes, and we've only twenty minutes to take the air before going to a luncheon party."

Auguste rose, offered her his right arm, and the two of them joined the promenade. The comments that trailed after them only increased their enjoyment of their playacting.

"Think they're brother and sister?"

"Wonder when the poor mites had their last meal."

"Shouldn't be allowed to ape the upper classes. Making fun, that's what."

Astair's face flushed. "That one," she said, "wouldn't know quality from trash if you buried her nose in it. As for pitying the 'poor mites'—well, they can just keep their damned pity to themselves!"

Auguste heard a sound sadder than anger in her tones. He seized her hand and urged her forward, out of the park, down the three blocks to the Ecole Bernard. He took out his key.

"Auguste!" Astair exclaimed. "You are already master of the house?" She was laughing now.

He ushered her into the kitchen and gestured widely to include the whole room. Then he opened the refrigerator.

"You mean we can have what we want? As much as we want?"

For reply Auguste took the butter and cheese from the shelves, extracted the bread from a cupboard, and put it all together on the table.

"Oh, no! Let me!" Astair cried. "You be the father, just home from a very tiring day at the Musée de l'Art Moderne. I go there often to get warm, and I even like some of the things on the walls. The paintings of the country mostly. There's one of a village in a grassy valley where the houses are so real you can make yourself small and walk among them. Even the well has water in it." She brushed back her hair with the palms of her hands and then smoothed her skirt. "But I mustn't keep you waiting."

She washed three potatoes and began to peel them. She glanced again into the bin. Hiding her action from Auguste, she hurriedly took out eight more and dropped them into the sink. Taking a sizable pot from the top of the stove, she brought it to the basin and filled it from the faucet. Almost furtively she plopped the eleven potatoes into the pot.

She turned to find Auguste beside her, his look questioning.

"There are plenty of apples, too, and bread and everything," she said urgently. "Oh, Auguste, let me invite them—Francois, Jerome and Thomas! What they eat in a day, if they're lucky, you could put in your pocket and have room left over. Please!"

For a moment Auguste's face reflected worry. Madame Louva had left him the responsibility of the house. But he couldn't resist the force of Astair's pleading. He nodded.

The girl hopped for joy. "You break the eggs—we're going to have a giant omelette—and wash the apples and get out the knives and forks and by the time you do all that I'll be back with our comrades. Get busy now!"

She dashed from the house.

Five minutes later the troupe of boys followed Astair into the hallway. Auguste beckoned them into the kitchen.

"What's up?" asked Francois, reaching for the loaf of bread.

Astair caught his hand. "No—you have to wait. This is a party and we'll all behave like ladies and gentlemen."

"Lady and gentlemen," corrected Jerome.

She glanced at the company. "You're a grimy lot. It shows inside a real house. Auguste, you take them to the bathroom. They'll have to wash before lunch."

There was a communal groan, but the boys willingly followed their host from the room.

They returned looking rather sheepish to be so unusually clean. Thomas was whispering to Francois, "There were eight towels. I counted them."

"Hope you didn't use them all," said Astair.

"No, just one. Came out kind of gray."

"Sit down. Some of you get extra chairs from the dining room." She seated herself beside Auguste. "Now we'll just have to be patient until the potatoes cook." She gazed at the silent group. "Well, talk, can't you?"

No one offered a subject.

"Then we'll sing. Jerome, you choose. I noticed how many people you had listening to you last Saturday outside the cinema. The sad song got the most applause."

"And most of what I collected," said the boy. "Want me to start?"

Astair clapped her hands.

Jerome's eyes became distant as he began to sing in a husky baritone threaded with sweetness.

> Slit my gullet like a pullet,
> Even though you twist the knife
> He who sings has a lock on life.
>
> When all is lost but this sinner's ghost
> I'll climb the hole from underground
> And what I gave will see me crowned.
>
> So sing, Jerome, sing on alone,
> Your certain home, sing fair or faint,
> Is paradise and you're a saint.

For a few seconds there was no sound in the room but the bubbling of the pot. Then the talk began.

"Bravo, Jerome!"

"Haven't cried so hard since the rat ate my feet off." Francois's mockery was admiring.

"Remember last Sunday when that old lady gave you her scarf full of holes?" asked Thomas.

"How about that drunk we found in the alley last week?" joined Jerome.

There was general laughter.

"Tell Astair and Auguste!"

Jerome took up the story. "Well, we were going to take a few francs from his wallet—he was about half there and most amiable toward us and the garbage can he was propped against. One of us had already extracted the wallet—Thomas did it—and was about to divide up the money when the man came to and said he wanted a share.

He insisted it be a fair and equal division so Thomas handed his wallet back, didn't you, *mon vieux*?"

"Certainly. Nothing else to do," Thomas replied. "Too weird entirely for anything more sensible."

"So," went on Jerome, "the man pulled out a fat packet of francs and proceeded to count out four piles on the pavement. Then he looked at us—sort of the way a little kid looks when he's happy—and we all forgot what we were. We forgot together. We gathered all the money into one heap and stuffed it back into his wallet." He paused. "Except for twenty francs for our dinner."

"Then what did you do?" asked Astair impulsively.

"We found his address on his business card, got him on his feet and put him into a taxi."

"I love that story," the girl exclaimed. "And now we can eat!"

Ten minutes later they were all concentrating on their plates filled with eggs and potatoes.

"You know," said Astair, "your table manners are disgraceful. You don't have to gulp it down like dogs. We've lots left—cheese and apples for dessert and all afternoon to eat it."

"Just as you wish, madame," said Francois, crooking his little finger and taking mouse-size bites. The others mimicked him and fell into fits of laughter.

In half an hour the food was gone.

"I'll wash the dishes later," Astair announced. "Where's Jerome?"

"Gone exploring, I expect," said Francois.

Astair ran to the doorway. "Oh, no, he won't!" She leaped up the stairs two at a time and overtook the boy halfway up. "Come back here. This isn't our house!"

But before she could pull him down into the hall, Auguste passed her, beckoning the others to follow.

He flung open the door of the studio. For a few seconds they all stared in at the great mirrors full of clouds and sky, reflected from the windows opposite.

"It's like a painting that moves," said Jerome, nearly whispering. He was shoved from behind.

A sudden hilarity seized them all and they began to caper and hop and make faces at themselves in the glass.

"Monkeys, all of you!" said Astair.

Someone pulled her into a whirl around the room.

Only Auguste remained motionless, watching.

Chasing each other, colliding and pummeling, they raced and danced until Thomas stumbled and they ended up breathless, all in a laughing heap.

Astair cried out, "I know what! Let's go to the zoo!"

A cheer of approval met her suggestion and they streamed down the staircase and into the corridor.

"You go ahead," she said. "I have to clean up here first."

"We'll help you."

"No—that's the hostess's job. See you in half an hour by the elephants."

When they had gone Astair discovered that Auguste, too, had chosen to stay. He had just turned on the hot water faucet when he heard the front door open. Heavy, familiar steps were approaching the kitchen.

⌒ 10 ⌒

Madame Louva!

She slammed her black handbag onto the table. *"C'est incroyable!"* she shouted. "Unbelievable!"

Auguste and Astair were frozen.

"I come back early, my day ruined, my sister gone to care for a sick cousin, not needing or wanting my company, and what do I find? My kitchen wrecked, my food practically gone, and, worst of all, my house entertaining an assembly of street rats! Oh, yes, I saw them leave. They tore down the street as though chased by the devil himself. That was me, of course, and I wish right now I had a forked tail! I'd whip you with it, both of you!"

"They're not rats!" said Astair. "They're my friends!"

"That doesn't surprise me," countered the furious housekeeper. "You're no better than the pack of them." Madame Louva's face was mottled and her raised hands were fists. Astair tensed, prepared to duck a blow.

Auguste slid between them, as if to shield Astair.

This seemed to fuel her fury. "No need to protect her

from me. I know her and I'm not about to slap her. It's not my way, though *le Bon Dieu* knows I'd like to!" She focused her anger on the boy. "And you, my fine young cockerel! You arrive, dumb, hungry, with your bones showing through your skin and we take you in though for all we know you might at any moment be at our throats. We trust you, I trust you and see what happens to that trust!"

Astair was filling the dishpan with soap and water.

"Touch nothing, you young tramp! Nothing! I'll not have your filth in my kitchen, and if you ever come back, so much as put your toe in the door, I'll take a switch to you. Now go!"

Astair escaped, wordless.

Madame Louva glared toward the doorway. She did not look directly at Auguste again but the pitch of her anger lowered into severity. "As for you, take yourself upstairs to your room. It is Monsieur Bernard who'll give you your walking papers, not I."

She did not watch his slow ascent.

Auguste stared at the floor, but instead of seeing the scarred, unwaxed boards of the attic he envisioned those of a stage, a stage he would never perform on.

The cat tried to squeeze into his lap, then slipped down and sat contemplating the boy with unblinking eyes.

Unfastening the pouch from inside his shirt, Auguste drew out the little velvet box and, opening it almost timidly, as though he expected to find it empty, he looked at the medallion. Why hadn't its brilliance dimmed? Why did the star deep in the center of the sapphire still shine for him, still speak of his dead teacher? He had failed, finally and irretrievably, failed himself—but more terribly, failed Hercule Hilaire, the man who had given him both his love and his magic. Then the figures of Monsieur Bernard, who had seemed somehow sent to him from his old master, and Madame Louva, who had so recently made him welcome, entered his mind and he grieved, his sorrow so far entrenched within him no tears reached his eyes.

He shut the box, blanking the medallion from his sight. He would never look at it again. This bright star was not destined for him. He tucked it back into its hiding place. He held out his hands as though they still contained the now alien treasure, and at that instant the cat jumped into them, balancing the length of its body along Auguste's arms.

The boy bent his head and kissed it between the ears; then he gently placed it on the floor and got up. He must leave before Monsieur Bernard returned, but first there was one last act to perform. Carefully he closed the door on the cat. Someone would hear its meowing and release it into the streets.

The studio was filled with the violet light of dusk. He moved into it slowly, formally, as if enacting a ceremony, a grave and practiced ritual. He faced himself in the mirrors, acknowledging his image, but as a stranger. Gradually, as he retreated, small step by small step backward and away, his own feeling of farewell crescendoed. When he reached the doorway he stilled the statement, and the violet light deepened into blue.

Shutting the studio door, he descended the stairs as noiselessly as the cat might have, but he was not to escape.

Madame Louva was blocking the hall. "Oh, no," she said, "it's not going to be that easy. You come right into this kitchen where I can watch you. Monsieur Bernard will be back before too long now." From habit she studied him. Today he seemed somehow strung like a marionette as he stood slackly in the corner by the stove, a marionette that offered no more promise of movement than a bundle of sticks.

She poured a cup of coffee for herself, and then a second. As though to someone with a sickness, she handed it to him, her gesture tentative. He folded his hands around the warmth of it but did not drink.

The two of them heard the turn of Monsieur Bernard's key in the lock. He entered and sat down heavily in the nearest chair. His face was chalked by exhaustion. For a few seconds he rested his head in his hands, and a long sigh came from behind them.

Then he straightened. "Very strenuous, the country. I'd rather carpenter a theatre all by myself than stumble about in the woods or compliment the neighbor's cows." He rubbed at his eyes.

Auguste moved toward the door but the housekeeper barred his exit. "Monsieur, may I get you a glass of wine to refresh you?"

He shook his head emphatically. "Too much champagne entirely, all day. Bragge and Heloise quite enjoyed themselves but I kept thinking of the school and the coming Christmas performance. There's time, but not too much. A month isn't forever."

Madame Louva cut through his worrying. "You should get your rest, monsieur, but first I must tell you what happened here today. I'll be brief."

As promised, the account of her ravaged kitchen, her astounded sense of betrayal by Auguste, the desecration of her trust in him, was kept within the boundaries of brevity, but the fervor of the telling was at such a pitch that Auguste felt himself shrinking with each added phrase.

Monsieur Bernard was so absorbed in his housekeeper's emotions he did not know that a smile was beginning to curl his mouth upward. When she had come to the end, he glanced at Auguste's abject expression of apology and burst into laughter.

"Forgive me," he said, still unable to muffle his amusement, "please forgive me, my own dear guardian angel, but why not? It only meant that the young culprit here felt so much at home he invited all his friends in, and if they are urchins then so much the better. I expect they thoroughly delighted in what they ate and perhaps for once had enough."

"Mercy on us!" she exclaimed. "To think you would tolerate those dirty creatures in your lovely house!"

He got up and, putting one arm around her shoulders, affectionately pinched her cheek. "Now, now, nothing tragic has taken place. Let's just forget it, shall we?" He turned to Auguste. "As for you, just continue to make yourself useful and I'll be content. However, no further invitations are to be issued without the consent of the head of the household." He smiled again at Madame Louva, who was so pleased at this unusual attention from her beloved patron she had dismissed the entire incident.

Monsieur Bernard went to the doorway. "*Bonne nuit* to both of you. Sleep well." With a wave of his hand he disappeared up the stairs.

Auguste, his face still unrelieved of its distress, waited as if struck into stone.

The housekeeper, determined to conserve at least a semblance of sternness, looked at the boy a moment, long enough to increase his nervousness. Then she spoke. "Well, if he can forgive you, I guess I must too, but not in the same spirit. I want no more such nonsense. Is that understood? And for your penance you will give the studio such a cleaning as it has never had before. It is to be complete before the practice hour, and that means you will have to get up well before dawn. Be good for you. Now good night." She murmured a *"Bonne nuit"* under her breath as she watched him race up the stairs. If he had heard, he would have recognized in her tones an admission of her affection for him.

But Auguste was not to sleep that night without a more open expression of affection. The moment he lay down, the cat curled up beside him, its ears tickling Auguste's chin.

❧ 11 ❧

Auguste had just finished the windowpanes as the first six students straggled into the studio. They chattered among themselves, only one nodding a greeting to him. The rest followed on their heels with Philippe last, pausing on the threshold for dramatic effect.

His *"Bonjour"* to the group was as formal as if he were the master.

"Oh, stop playacting," called one.

"Take off the crown!"

"Pretend you're like the rest of us. Try, anyway."

A knot of friendly tussling crowded Philippe. When he had enough of the shoving, he reached for Auguste. "So our little *chiffonnier* is still with us!" he jeered. "The little ragman himself."

"Doesn't look much like a ragman to me," said one of the girls.

"Be quiet!" commanded Philippe. "I'm the leader here."

"Who says?"

"Because I'm the best and I'll get the main part in the new show."

Suddenly the class stillled, for Monsieur Bernard's footsteps were audible on the stairs. The boys and girls hurried to position themselves in an orderly row at the bar.

As the teacher entered they answered his *"Bonjour"* almost in unison. "How goes it this fine day?" he asked.

Little murmurs of response stirred the silence.

"Please, everyone sit on the floor. We have only a few weeks to prepare it and I expect absolute dedication and excellence on the final performance. I will, as always, consider suggestions, if thoughtfully made. I will not tolerate inattention, lateness or laziness. We are gathered here to work, are we not?"

Prompt and earnest "Yes, monsieur"s came from everybody but Philippe. He had separated himself from the others, as if superior to them.

Monsieur Bernard allowed a moment's silence to emphasize his words. "Now!" He clapped his hands. "To our daily exercises!"

When they had completed the routines at the bar and formed three lines across the room, Auguste, who had been leaning against a rear window, slowly stood straight and began to move with the others.

It was Philippe, glancing back, who first noticed him. "What's he doing in our class? Look at him. Think he belonged!"

Monsieur Bernard put his forefinger to his lips for silence. "Let him be as one of you. It does no one harm. That backbend again, please. Better control this time."

Two hours later the class was dismissed. Philippe signaled Raymond and Jean-Louis to stay. "I tell you I'm tired of the master defending that walking garbage with no tongue in his head," he said angrily.

"Oh, I'm sure he has a tongue," said Raymond.

Philippe slapped him across the mouth. "That was just a figure of speech, you little fool. And don't interrupt again."

Raymond was sniveling. He wiped his eyes with the back of one hand.

"Stop that!" said Jean-Louis. "Sometimes you act like a three-year-old."

"Listen to me," said Philippe, his smile sly. "I've got an idea how to have some fun with the dummy."

The three boys closed in, their heads touching. Philippe continued in a whisper. "You see, he's got a cat in his room."

At four o'clock that afternoon, Madame Louva sent Auguste from the house, saying, "I've kept you at it long enough. I believe your lesson is learned. Enough is enough. Go along now and see what the world around us has to offer you." She wanted to give him a few francs to spend, but she resisted this spoiling and instead smoothed down the ragged collar of his shirt and unnecessarily resettled his jacket on his shoulders.

The boy hurried out to find Astair. Her chalk mark was missing from the baker's stoop, so going to the basement room, he tapped on the one window, so grimy it was opaque. The door opened a crack.

"Oh, it's you!" Astair's face was quickly joyful. She joined Auguste on the sidewalk. "What's your plan for the afternoon?"

He danced a little jig.

"Then I'll play the tambourine." She lifted off the lid of a trash can and, finding the handle of a small broom in the rubbish, began to beat on the lid in time to Auguste's steps.

The two of them pranced down the street and around the corner.

At the end of an hour they had collected a handful of centimes and five francs from shoppers who stopped to watch Auguste's dancing and miming.

Auguste carefully counted out the coins, giving Astair an equal share.

"But I've done nothing but bang out the rhythms you danced to! Here, take back half of what I have."

Auguste refused.

"Then I must perform, too." Her eyes clouded, as if her spirit had retreated far away where no one could follow. "I heard a song when I was young," she said in a voice so low Auguste could scarcely hear it.

He sat on the curb at her feet and looked up expectantly.

Astair, still so removed she might have been a statue of herself, folded her hands together tightly like a child and began to sing.

> *Que tu sois libre de peur*
> *(Par instants enfant de la nuit)*
> *Je te donne mon coeur,*
> *Oiseau chantant*
> *Petite soeur en plumes.*
> *Ecoute-lui*
> *Sa voix allume*
> *La tristesse de ton soir*
> *Et tout ce qui est noir*
> *Devient le jour*
> *Par son amour.*
> *Que tu sois libre de peur*
> *Je te donne mon coeur.*

That you be free of fear
(Sometimes a child of the night)
I give you my heart,
A singing bird
A little sister in feathers.
Listen to her
Her voice illumines
The sadness of your evening
And all that is dark
Will become the day
By her love.
That you be free of fear
I give you my heart.

At the closing of the last note an old woman took out her handkerchief and wiped her cheeks. A man cleared his throat. Another hacked out a delayed cough. Three people, instead of throwing coins on the pavement, handed the girl their contributions, and the little crowd of people moved away.

Still Astair seemed lost in what she had sung. Quickly Auguste encircled her in his arms. The gesture lasted no longer than an instant.

She smiled. Then, glancing at what she held in her hand, exclaimed, "Oh, look, Auguste! We've ten francs more!" She gave him five.

Auguste pointed in the direction of the school, answered her smile and raced away.

First he went to the *crémerie*, where he bought a bottle of milk, then to the fish stand, where he bought five fresh sardines wrapped in a paper packet. Entering the house a few moments later, he encountered Philippe and his two comrades

"Where's that nasty smell coming from?" taunted Philippe, winking at the others.

Auguste ignored them and took the stairs two at a time in his eagerness to offer these treats to his cat. But when he opened the door and looked in, no cat greeted him. The last faded shafts of sunlight speared the emptiness of his room. Dropping the food on the table, he frantically searched the attic, behind the trunks, even in the crevices of the stacked wood. No cat.

He ran down the stairs to the front door. The three boys were lolling outside on the front steps.

"Lost something?" asked Jean-Louis.

"Something furry?" echoed Raymond.

Auguste did not miss the malice so evident in their tones.

"Put it in the well on its way to hell!" chanted Philippe.

Auguste charged him, but before he could land a blow the other two had seized him by the arms, pinning them behind his back. Jean-Louis twisted his wrist and held it. Auguste managed to make his face a mask against the pain.

Philippe finally motioned for them to release Auguste. "He won't try anything, not while there are three of us. Don't worry," he said to his silent opponent. "Nothing's happened to your alley cat. Just took it for a long, long walk, far enough to lose it."

Auguste turned from them and reentered the house, his shoulders bent forward as though he were suddenly old. He climbed very slowly up and into the vacant studio. He sat in the middle of the floor, closing his eyes against the sight of himself in the mirrors. He heard Madame Louva calling him. He smelled the rising scents of her cooking but he did not stir. He seemed to become the color of the pale last light of day, as transparent as the blue air around him.

Then, as if summoned by someone not there, he got to his hands and knees and began to move. He prowled, he stalked, he licked the length of one leg, never touching it. The movements were mournful, sorrowing. The moment ended and Auguste lay back onto the floor in seeming sleep, though his eyes stared at the ceiling.

He did not see the tall shadow in the doorway, did not know his transformation into a cat had been witnessed. There was a sound of clapping. Auguste looked toward it and sprang to his feet. There was silence between them. Monsieur Bernard's gaze was so intense it was as though he were etching in his mind the boy before him, line by line, so as never to lose him.

He broke the concentration with a smile. "It is time for us to talk," he said, "or, rather, for me to talk, though what you told me about a cat was more than eloquent." He lowered himself to the floor and sat cross-legged, beckoning Auguste to join him.

The boy obeyed but at a distance of several yards.

"Madame Louva," he began, "tells me you were a foundling, grew up on a farm. She is a sentimental woman, my dear housekeeper, but she often intuitively arrives at the truth. She believes you were driven out of your village, that they feared you. Was she correct?"

Auguste nodded, giving nothing of himself.

"And then?"

The boy flattened his hands and then made a kind of swimming gesture, as if sweeping himself free of what had come next.

Monsieur Bernard did not misunderstand. "Well, your past is of no importance, except to you. What is important

70

to me is your talent. As I told you before, I would like you to join my classes."

Auguste straightened quickly and for an instant he started to rise. His eyes were no longer lacquered by sadness.

"I am curious about one thing," continued the master. "You must have had some training, at least in the concept of mime."

Auguste felt the touch of the pouch that contained the medallion against his skin but gave no response to Monsieur Bernard's inquiry. He would not expose, even to the kindness of this great teacher, the mysterious heritage given him by the dying Hilaire. His strength lay in the guarding of these gifts of love and faith.

Monsieur Bernard sighed. "Perhaps you are that most rare of all, a natural." He searched the guarded face of the strange, silent boy, feeling him so much farther away than the few yards that separated them. Why did this boy remind him of his own past? What was the alliance? Where? He put aside the impossibility of his random thoughts and addressed his next words to the present.

"To business, *mon élève*, for my pupil you have become. Are you willing to work?"

The quick light in the boy's eyes was answer enough.

"I take no one who is not willing to make this promise to me. Life is a brief journey and to become an artist is a long road. I know. I've no time to waste on the less than serious."

Auguste rose and stood rigidly at attention.

"But, *mon petit*, your hands are shaking!" Monsieur Bernard stood, too. He approached the boy. "Does this then mean so much to you?"

Auguste bowed from the waist, honoring the man in

front of him. Monsieur Bernard held out his hand and the boy took it. Both understood that this was their contract, promise to promise.

"Now we must go to dinner. Madame Louva is probably already in a temper at our lateness. She forgives me much, the dear woman."

They hurried to the dining room. The three boarders were seated, but at the entrance of their master they got to their feet and remained standing until he had seated himself at the head of the table.

As Auguste sat down across from him, Philippe nudged Jean-Louis, who snickered behind one hand.

Madame Louva came in with a steaming casserole which she set before her patron. "Sorry you missed the soup, monsieur."

"It is indeed punishment to be deprived of it," said Monsieur Bernard, his smile teasing.

The housekeeper was obviously mollified by the implied apology and took her chair at the other end of the table.

After the stew was served the two adults talked of other concerns. Philippe made several mewing sounds at Auguste, who did not acknowledge these attentions.

When the cheese and fruit were eaten Monsieur Bernard raised his hand. "I have an announcement to make," he said. "As of tomorrow Auguste becomes a member of our troupe. You three already know my disciplines. Auguste will soon have learned them."

There was a grunt from Philippe.

Monsieur Bernard understood its meaning and continued. "I realize that Auguste comes from a background very different from yours. That difference, as well as Auguste's physical difference, can cause dissension. Listen

72

well. I will not countenance any interruption of what we are all here for—the excellence of our work. Is that understood?"

There was a ragged murmur of "Yes, *Monsieur le maître.*"

Their teacher relaxed his strictness. "Let me tell you what happened to me when a mouse came onstage with me." The story, when completed, brought them all into laughter.

"Now," said Madame Louva, "out, all of you. Up to bed. It is late and we all have tomorrow, God be thanked."

All the way up to his attic Auguste sang within himself the words "We all have tomorrow."

๑ 12 ๑

That first week of daily exercises was difficult for Auguste. The many months of wandering, of scrounging for food wherever opportunity offered it—in work or begging, or scraps from refuse cans—the cold that had stiffened him, all these had taken flexibility and power from his muscles.

Each evening after he had washed the supper dishes for Madame Louva and wiped the counters clean, he would climb to his attic. There, despite the aching of his body, he would once more go through the set of disciplines before he flung himself on his cot, sometimes forced to wait a few minutes for the will to pull the blanket up over his tiredness.

During those first days Philippe and his cohorts imitated behind Monsieur Bernard's back the mistakes of the new pupil. They laughed when leg cramps lamed him.

Madame Louva was aware of this mockery but she did not interfere. Instead, she would encourage him by putting a little packet of chocolate in his jacket pocket or leaving an apple in his room to surprise him. Each morning when the others had breakfasted and gone, she sat him down at the kitchen table and gave him a bowl of porridge, thickly coated with sugar and cream. She could see the thanks in his eyes.

Each Tuesday and Thursday, when Auguste was permitted three hours off, he arranged to meet Astair. But a Thursday came when under the tree where Auguste had once placed his vanished cat there was no Astair.

He searched the park, thinking she might have met a friend, but nowhere did he glimpse the light grace of her or hear her sparrowlike voice.

He ran from the park and down the streets to her basement room. He did not pause at the dirt-filmed window or knock at the small door under the stoop. He turned the knob. It wobbled in his grip and then released the latch.

Inside, he saw only grayed gloom. Then forms began to emerge: the table, an unlighted kerosene lamp, the chair, and in the far corner the narrow window seat heaped with what seemed to be old clothes.

Tiptoeing across the uneven boards of the floor, he went to the ledge and found what he had expected—Astair. Her eyelids were swollen; a round spot of red, like on a clown's mask, marked each cheek. Her smile was strained.

"Don't be so sad," she said in a small voice. "It's just my rheumatism come back. I'm used to it—too many winters. I can still sing even if I can't dance yet."

Auguste sat down on the chair close to her bed. He drew the stained old quilt up to her chin and then pretended to spoon something into her mouth.

She smiled again. "The boys bring me tidbits now and then, as much as they can spare. Don't worry. I'll be up

75

and out in just a few more days." She was gazing now at the viewless window as if seeing something Auguste could not see.

"I remember things, lying here," she began. "Things I forget when I'm occupied with the world. Then I don't have time for remembering."

Auguste opened his hands as though waiting to receive her memories.

She nodded. "I'll tell you one. It's my favorite. I must have been very young because someone put me on a table and I had no way of getting down. There was a vase of flowers next to me, roses I think or maybe that's just because I like to remember them as roses. Then someone who smelled exactly like the flowers lifted me up and held me and sort of rocked me back and forth."

He tapped her hand and pointed to himself in order to get her attention. Then he stood before her, seeming to expand into a figure wider and more solid. He made a cradle of his arms and, so slowly he was almost not moving, he swung his body to and fro, his face downward, cherishing what he held.

For many moments she watched him until, at last, the gentle repetition soothed her into sleep.

Immediately Auguste let himself out into the street. A few minutes later he was on the busiest corner of the nearest boulevard. He capered and clowned, collecting coins as they were dropped at his feet.

Late that afternoon he had sixty francs. Then he bought two apples, a pear and a box of thick crackers at the grocer's and had just enough money left to add a tiny pink cake from the bakery. He let himself back into Astair's room and set out the food. She was still sleeping.

He leaned down and stroked her hair with a touch as light as a moth. Then he hurried back to the school.

"Exactly on the hour," Madame Louva greeted him, "and most fortuitously arrived. You four boys will eat in the kitchen tonight, and you, Auguste, will be my assistant in the dining room. Monsieur Bernard invited Madame Trollant and Monsieur Bragge for dinner and my rheumatism is plaguing me today."

Astair and the housekeeper, young and old, were sharing the same discomforts. Auguste wished he could tell Madame Louva about the dank cellar he had just left and the plight of the girl in it. But he remembered Madame Louva's fierce words when she had walked into her ruined kitchen, finding Astair. "If you so much as put your toe in the door, I'll take a switch to you!"

His wish died.

Supper over, the others gone to their rooms, Auguste became the server of the four courses to the guests after being meticulously coached by the housekeeper. Once Monsieur Bernard smiled at him, as though to salute the success of his efforts. Monsieur Bragge ignored his presence, and all he received from Philippe's mother was a single sniff of disapproval.

When he had taken in the cognac and the tray of crystal glasses, he leaned against the frame of the kitchen door and watched Madame Louva lower herself into a chair. "Thank you, *mon enfant*. I don't believe I could have done without you tonight."

He put before her a smaller glass and the bottle of calvados that was her occasional refreshment.

She poured out a portion and sipped it. "Do you know why I prefer this above all the others?" she asked. "Be-

77

cause it comes from my home country, Normandy, made from the apples I helped harvest when I was young. That was a lovely time. But you must rest. Off to bed with you! I'll just sit here awhile and converse with my ghosts.'

He bowed his good-night, but as he was about to start up the stairs Monsieur Bragge's voice stopped him.

"Time to be practical," the manager was saying. "My theatre can't put on the Christmas show for free. You owe three weeks' rehearsal time from last month as it is."

Madame Trollant's voice cut in. "And me, *maître*, what can you expect from me? Without my help only the good Lord knows where the school would be today."

"In the streets, most likely," chimed in Bragge.

Monsieur Bernard spoke next. "What's to be done? I confess I am at the end of my resources. I can pay Madame Louva and purchase the food for my boarders and even make the rent, but as for anything substantial left over! I might as well try to mine the moon for silver."

"There is one solution," said Bragge, "one I have reminded you of more often than I care to count. You must play again. No, listen to me. You have a reputation, a great one. The box office receipts would give you more than sufficient funds to pay your bills and replenish your bank account."

Auguste was suddenly filled with pain as real as Astair's, as Madame Louva's. His master's tones were sad, hurting Auguste. "Bragge," said the old man, "you know I can't. I am not what I was."

"And who will know the difference? Even if they do, Parisians can be kind when honoring an artist they have so long applauded and admired. I know them. So do you."

"I know the difference," countered the master mime. "I

78

cannot offer them less for the very reason that once I did give them my best."

Now Madame Trollant broke in. "You are a fool, whatever kind of artist you are or have been. You know this is true. Admit it. Suppose I withhold my support?" The reality of the threat towered within her voice.

Monsieur Bragge answered for him. "The school will close."

"And what will become of you?" the woman drove on.

"Of me?" The mime's tones faltered then, but he drew from somewhere deep inside himself a last flare of vitality. His next words came resonant and sure. "Madame Louva's sister in the Loire Valley has a room she will let me live in. She has promised it."

"Oh my God!" spluttered Bragge. "You in a village with everybody staring and whispering whenever you go to the one café for an infrequent glass of wine? If you can afford it."

Auguste heard the prediction with anguish. His own beloved master, Hercule Hilaire, had retired to live and die far from any friends, feared by the peasants, trapped in loneliness with only the yellowed programs piled in a trunk for company.

Monsieur Bragge would not let go. "You existing in a provincial quagmire?" He was almost shouting. "Better cut your throat first!"

At this Auguste felt someone push past him. It was Madame Louva. She stood, her hands on her hips, filling the threshold of the dining room. "I heard that," she said, "and I'll have no more of it!"

Auguste no longer bothered to hide.

Madame Trollant's expression was icy. "Keep your place, my good woman, or you'll lose it!"

The housekeeper's mouth tightened. "That will be for Monsieur Bernard to say!" She returned to the kitchen.

"Well, monsieur," said Madame Trollant, "I hope you are able to exercise better control of your students than you do of your servants. What an exhibition! And now, so that the matter is plainly spelled out between us—Philippe is getting bored with his lessons. The new show will be his last."

"Yes," said Bragge, "he's not star quality, as we all realize."

Philippe's mother was now ugly with anger. "You keep out of this! I will back you once more, Bernard. After that—" She allowed the future to dangle in their faces. "*Bonsoir*, gentlemen, though God knows it has not been a good evening."

Auguste retired to the kitchen, where he and the housekeeper shared a long look, not needing speech to express their sadness.

⌒ 13 ⌒

Auguste indulged in a small ceremony each morning in the privacy of his attic. Before he did his first set of exercises, he hung Hilaire's medallion on a nail over his bed. When his routine was done, he replaced it in the hiding place under his shirt. Perhaps now, he thought, he was gradually beginning to earn it, as Monsieur Hilaire had said he must. Sometimes he even imagined he could hear his teacher's voice, approving, correcting, and always loving.

On the start of this particular day, the sky was intervalled with blue and gray, and Auguste suddenly wanted to stretch, to lift himself into the freedom of it. He pushed up the skylight and emerged into another Paris. Why had he never ventured here before? The peaks of hundreds of slate roofs, unevenly topped with chimneypots, horizoned the sky. Thousands of windows gleamed back at him, round ones like his own, square ones, some linked by lines of laundry. A world of windows. Wood-smoke from some of the chimneys drifted southward on the cool wind, scenting the air, and Auguste could imagine the fireplaces below and the families around them.

Just as he was about to return to his attic to conceal the medallion, three birds rose in a flutter and winged past him. A shadow detached itself from a neighboring chimney, and he saw the cause of their alarm. It was a cat, his cat, washing itself in the thin sunlight.

Auguste waved. He wished he had something with which to make a noise. He tried clapping his hands together but still the animal did not look up. There was nothing to do but to cross to where it was. Cautiously he climbed all the way through the skylight.

At this moment Raymond wandered idly into the kitchen saying, "Where's Auguste?"

Madame Louva, busy peeling turnips, merely remarked, "I don't know Why?"

"Just wondered."

"That's something new," commented the housekeeper "You three never talk to him or try to make him feel at home. Why?"

"He's a dummy. Why bother?"

Madame Louva turned to him and Raymond knew the signs of a scolding, so he quickly excused himself and ran upstairs On his way to his room it occurred to him that he had never seen Auguste's attic. He called to Philippe to join him, and soundlessly the two boys ascended the final flight of stairs. Philippe motioned to Raymond to knock on the door.

There was no response.

"Come on!" said Philippe. "He's probably out on the street where he belongs."

The two of them entered.

Raymond was the first to see it. "Look!" he cried, star·

tled into loudness. "Just look at that!" He was pointing to
the glow of gold and sapphire that hung over Auguste's
bed.

"*Zut alors!* What the devil! Where do you suppose he
got it?"

"Stole it, of course," said Raymond importantly. "But
where would he even get to see such a thing? It's made of
real jewels!"

"I know that," said Philippe, miffed at being caught in
any attitude but indifference "My mother has lots of
them."

"I'll take it," Raymond announced. "How could he ever
accuse anybody? No tongue to do it with, and besides,
he's peasant class. No one would believe it's his."

Philippe leaped onto the cot and reached for the medallion. "No, you don't, Raymond! It's mine!"

Raymond, seeing the prize hung about Philippe's neck,
was furious. He shoved the larger boy onto the floor.

Philippe countered by pulling Raymond down and rolling him over onto his back. Then he gripped his head on
both sides and banged it against the floor. Raymond
kicked hard with his heels, trying to dislodge his attacker.

In three minutes they heard the housekeeper on the first
landing. She was calling, "What's the rumpus up there?
Come down or I'm coming up!"

Philippe released the boy underneath him. "We've got
to get out of here fast. Come on—through the skylight."

Raymond followed, waiting his chance to snatch the
medallion from Philippe's neck.

They crawled onto the slanted roof. "We can get down
the fire escape," said Philippe, "and go back in as if we'd
been for a walk."

"Not until you give me that medal. I saw it first. It's mine!"

"Don't be an idiot!"

"You copped it from me, I tell you!" Raymond was nearly hysterical. "And furthermore, I'm sick and tired of being called any old name you think up out of that sick brain of yours! I'm not an idiot!"

"Shut your mouth, idiot, stupid cow, butt of nothing!" jeered Philippe. "It belongs to me and that's the end of it!"

Neither noticed Auguste two chimneys away, now holding the cat safe in his arms.

Raymond aimed a blow at Philippe with his left fist and with his right hand tried to wrest the medallion from him.

Philippe smashed him viciously across the face.

Raymond staggered backward. His right foot slipped and before he could even cry out, his body arced into the air and down. Auguste could hear the thud as Raymond landed on his back, caught in a canvas awning.

Philippe scurried back through the skylight, rehung the medallion on the nail and, checking his speed, strolled into the studio, which was now filled with students. He mingled as though he had been there all the time with the others.

It was Auguste who, still clutching the cat, tore down the stairs and into the kitchen, waving wildly at Madame Louva and then tugging her out into the street.

"My God, child, what is the matter?" said the housekeeper. But her question was answered as she saw Raymond's sprawled body above her.

She screamed.

Almost instantly she was surrounded by people. The authoritative voice of an officer of the police bellowed,

"Stand back, please, everyone." He blew his whistle three times. A few moments later a low, dark car pulled up at the curb and two more officers climbed out.

The crowd had enlarged and the windows on both sides of the street were filled with men and women.

An ambulance had been summoned on the car radio. Its arrival beep alerted the entire neighborhood. Another official car slid to a halt in front of the school. A lean, long-nosed man not in uniform stepped out and was greeted respectfully by the other policemen. He consulted in undertones not audible to the crowd, and then addressed them.

"Who is in charge here? To whom does this boy belong?"

Madame Louva came forward, wringing her hands. "He's ours, *Monsieur l'inspecteur*. I mean he is a pupil of Monsieur Bernard, who runs a theatre school in this building."

"And you, madame, who are you?"

"I am the housekeeper, sir."

"And this one?" He indicated Auguste, who had his free arm around Madame Louva's waist.

"He's one of the students. He saw it first."

"We will now go inside," said the inspector. "I request that anyone not connected with this matter please disperse." He gestured to his inferiors to assume this responsibility and led the way into the house.

"But the boy!" said the housekeeper.

"He will be taken to the hospital. Please tell Monsieur Bernard and anyone else concerned I shall want to see them immediately." He entered the dining room. "This will do," he added and sat at the head of the table.

∽ 14 ∾

The interviews began with Monsieur Bernard giving the inspector information about the injured boy and his parents' address so they could be notified.

Gradually it was revealed that both Raymond and Philippe had been in the attic. Madame Louva saw to it that her suspicions were confirmed by directly accusing Philippe.

"And then?" said the officer from the Sûreté.

"We were just fooling around," said Philippe.

"You were present at the time of the accident?"

"No, monsieur," said Philippe firmly. "But he was." He pointed at Auguste.

"So?" The inspector's voice was cool. He looked at Auguste. "What have you to say to that?"

Monsieur Bernard intervened. "He is a mute, monsieur, but most intelligent. He will answer in his own way."

Auguste's reply was a nod.

Madame Louva gasped. "He wouldn't hurt a beetle, much less another person!" she exclaimed. "There is a terrible tangle here."

"And are you now conducting this interrogation, madame?" There was no mistaking the rebuke.

"I ask your pardon, *Monsieur l'inspecteur*," said the housekeeper, "but I know this boy."

"I will ask for your personal opinions, madame, when I require them." He turned to Jean-Louis. "And you? Where were you?"

"In my room, monsieur, studying."

Auguste saw a glance from Philippe to Jean-Louis that seemed to indicate disgust that his comrade hadn't provided him with an alibi.

The inspector was now making notations in a little book. "The background of the mute?" he asked Monsieur Bernard.

"We knew nothing of him when he came to us," said the teacher, "but we have found him both industrious and trustworthy."

The inspector hummed under his breath, his eyes speculative as he noted Auguste's worn clothes and thinness.

"Trustworthy!" Jean-Louis blurted out, stung by Philippe's disapproval. "Just tell how he invited all his street pals in when he was alone and in charge of the school!"

The inspector listened with some impatience to the account. Then he gave his attention once more to Philippe. "You may tell me what you know of this affair. Raymond was a good friend of yours?"

Philippe nodded and took center stage with ease. "Raymond and Auguste went up on the roof through the skylight. I stayed below in the room. I could hear them arguing—" Philippe faltered for just one instant, then continued. "I mean I could hear Raymond arguing about something he thought Auguste had stolen from him. Then

87

there was a complete silence. I guess that's when Auguste pushed Raymond off the roof."

"What nonsense!" interposed Madame Louva. "Those boys, Philippe, Raymond and Jean-Louis, never have anything to do with Auguste. Don't even speak to him at meals. Why would they have been together when it all happened?"

This time the inspector simply ignored the housekeeper. He now spoke to Monsieur Bernard. "I am familiar with your school and its fine reputation. Please believe that I realize a scandal will not profit you. I will keep this investigation as quiet as possible."

"I appreciate that, monsieur," said Monsieur Bernard, "and will cooperate wherever I am able."

The inspector turned to Philippe. "You are the son of Madame Philippe Trollant, are you not? I have had the honor of meeting your mother."

Philippe smiled. "And I know of you, *Monsieur l'inspecteur*. My mother has often spoken of you."

The officer could not help showing his pleasure. "Since you were not a witness, why do you believe it not to have been an accident? That is the impression you have given me."

Philippe took his time. He knew the theatrical effect of a pause in the right place. "Because, monsieur," he said, indicating Auguste, "this one hated Raymond. Raymond is rich and he as poor as dirt. Wandered in here like a stray dog."

"Then no one knows anything about him?" asked the inspector.

"No," said Monsieur Bernard quietly.

The inspector directed his next question to Madame

Louva. "And now, madame, what is your opinion of this—this unknown, this deformed child from nowhere?"

The housekeeper spoke without hesitation. "You will excuse me, *Monsieur l'inspecteur*, but he is in no way deformed, not in mind or body."

"I ask your pardon for my carelessness of expression," responded the inspector with some irony. "Defective, then."

"Granted. As to my opinion, for what it's worth, in this unequal existence where birth and money often take precedence over justice—"

"If you please, madame," interrupted the official. "This is not the moment for a discourse on human frailty. I shall appreciate pertinence and brevity in your replies."

"My judgment of the boy, Auguste, coincides exactly with that of Monsieur Bernard," Madame Louva said, and then snapped her mouth shut and crossed her arms.

The inspector closed his notebook and tucked his gold pen into his breast pocket. "Monsieur Bernard," he began thoughtfully, "since there were no proved witnesses to what happened, and since the mute is unable to offer verbal testimony, I believe I can predict with confidence that the incident will be termed a regrettable accident and the case terminated without any undue complications or further questioning of the parties concerned."

He glanced toward Philippe as he rose to his feet. "I would, however, like to offer you my considered advice on a related subject."

The housekeeper directed her gaze to the ceiling. Monsieur Bernard remained quite perfectly civil.

"In these days," the inspector went on somewhat pompously, "in these days of peril in the streets, of unbridled criminality, it is not advisable to befriend flotsam and jetsam of unknown origin, however compassionate one may be."

Madame Louva was now just outside the dining room, half facing the front door. Her intention was obvious. "I am certain, monsieur," she said, "that you are a man of many responsibilities and affairs more important than ours."

The man nodded in smug agreement. "I will notify you if there are problems, Monsieur Bernard, but expect no trouble." He extended his hand to the teacher, then to both Jean-Louis and Philippe. Auguste did not receive this courtesy.

"Bonjour, madame, messieurs," he added and left the house.

Madame Louva let out a long breath through her teeth. "With your permission, monsieur," she said to her patron, "I am in need of a glass of brandy."

"We'll all have one," said the teacher.

"Never in my life!" murmured the housekeeper as she went to get the glasses. "Never!"

Monsieur Bernard addressed the three boys. "Just one more word," he said. "I want no talk, no talk at all, outside this house about what happened here today. Understood?"

He waited for the boys to signal their consent with nods.

"The school will be closed today and tomorrow out of respect for Raymond's misfortune. I will relay any report on his condition as soon as possible."

The housekeeper returned with a tray set with the brandy and five glasses. She poured equal amounts.

Auguste, who all this time had been holding the cat, let the animal sniff the contents of his glass. Then he too sniffed at the rim.

"I wasn't aware," said Madame Louva, "that you had permission to bring a cat into the house, Auguste." She was smiling at the two of them.

Monsieur Bernard started to leave the room. "I must prepare an announcement to tack on the front door," he said. "To inform the other students." He disappeared.

Madame Louva returned to the kitchen and Auguste started up the stairs, Philippe and Jean-Louis directly behind him. He hoped to be free of them both as he reached the last flight, but Philippe pushed past him as he climbed to the attic.

﹏ 15 ﹏

Philippe was already inside, his back to the window, his features in shadow. Auguste had not prevented his entering.

There was something furtive about his visitor. His habitual arrogance was somehow flawed. Auguste instinctively touched the pouch that once again held the medallion.

The other boy did not miss the gesture. "I've decided to let you keep that, even if you did steal it. I want no part of the kind of bad luck it brought Raymond. I would make you tell me where it came from if you had a tongue."

Auguste swallowed.

Philippe snorted. "Oh, I'm aware you have one. It just doesn't work right." He looked around the attic room. "Why don't you pawn it and buy something decent to wear? Or, best of all, take a trip and never come back."

During Philippe's speech Auguste's stance had become stiffer and stiffer, his arms rigid at his sides, his head erect and still. His immobility was so absolute it acted upon Philippe like a threat. His next words were less bold. He took a very deep breath. "All right. I'll ask you right out! Where were you when it happened?"

There was not a quiver of a response from Auguste.

Philippe charged him, and before Auguste could defend himself had pinned his right arm behind his back and was pushing it upward.

Auguste's mouth opened in a kind of soundless scream. He jerked his head toward the skylight.

"Then you saw, didn't you?"

Auguste nodded violently and tried to twist free.

Philippe released him. Vibrancy returned to his voice. "You were on the roof, too. You saw what I am capable of and you know I'm dangerous. I don't really give a damn what happens to Raymond. Live or die, he will never breathe a word against me. That I can count on. But you, if you rat on me I'll expose the medal and claim you stole it, that it belongs to me. They'll believe me because they have to, because my mother controls this place and they'll put you in a house of correction so fast . . ." Philippe had glimpsed the cat just three feet away. He kicked out at the animal and the creature sprang into the air, howling.

Auguste's fists battered at Philippe's face, forcing him back into the hall. His mouth and chin reddened with the blood that poured from his nose and he turned and fled down the stairs. Hearing his mother's voice in the little parlor off the dining room, he burst in on her and the two men.

He allowed Madame Trollant to embrace him, carefully so as not to soil her dress, while Monsieur Bragge produced a handkerchief and held it to the boy's nose. "See what you've got in your attic?" Philippe's mother shouted at Monsieur Bernard. "A beast—a wild beast!"

Philippe's eyes were watering from the force of the blow.

"Look at him!" ranted Madame Trollant. "Brave as he is, the tears arrive!"

Monsieur Bragge removed the boy from his mother's arms and wiped his face somewhat roughly. "Stop sniveling and go wash yourself. The bleeding has terminated."

When Philippe went back upstairs, certain of the result of the incident, the theatre manager directed his anger to Monsieur Bernard. "The mute is evidently unbalanced. First the dubious accident of Raymond, and now this attack on Philippe. He's got to go."

"Either that," said Madame Trollant, "or the funds no longer exist! As of this very moment," she added, stamping her right foot on the last word.

Monsieur Bernard's eyes seemed to darken. He lifted his hands in a gesture of acceptance.

"I'll soon put him out," said Bragge.

"No," said the master mime firmly. "That's for me to do. What Madame Louva will say, I dread to hear. She's fond of the boy as I, too, am fond of him."

"Another example of poor judgment," snapped Madame Trollant. "Just see that it's done. I'll telephone later for confirmation. Tell Philippe I'll be sending over some bonbons for him by special messenger. He's especially partial to glazed chestnuts." She waved her fingertips at the two men and left the building.

Monsieur Bragge briefly pressed the teacher's shoulder to express his sympathy and followed her.

Monsieur Bernard seemed suddenly aged, weary beyond recovery. Then he slowly climbed the stairs to the second landing, calling upward, "Auguste, come down to the studio." The room was painfully bright with sunlight.

The instant the boy entered, Monsieur Bernard knew there was no necessity for speeches, no matter how kind. The boy came to stand almost beside the teacher, and the two of them looked into the facing mirror at each other. Auguste's reflection seemed outlined in light, as the reality of him was not.

Monsieur Bernard ached for this brave ghost, and at the back of his looking was the faint presence of a kind of recognition. Like a final, clarifying stroke of paint on a portrait the teacher was given the vision of himself when young, and the image superimposed itself over the actuality of the other in the mirror. For that instant the two, past and present, were one.

Auguste was very still, remembering his dead master, remembering how they too had once stood together in front of a mirror, their reflections becoming partners. This moment seemed a repetition of the same profound friendship.

Then the old man spoke, breaking the likenesses apart. "It saddens me to say what I must," he began, "but I am forced to send you away. It is not my choice, but it is either you or the theatre and I cannot make that sacrifice. The theatre is my life. Do you understand me?

"You do understand," said Monsieur Bernard, and there was no questioning in his voice.

Auguste bowed to the teacher's image in the glass.

"*Mon Dieu*," murmured Monsieur Bernard as if to himself, "but the boy is eloquent. I can feel his pain in my own heart."

Unable to continue, the master mime strode to the door, not intending to look back. Something, almost an invisible touch, turned him. He halted, shocked.

The boy had taken an object from beneath his clothing

and was holding it against his chest. His hands clenched a ribbon and from it hung the medallion, shining like a true star within the shadow of the boy.

"Not possible!" cried Monsieur Bernard. He crossed the few feet that separated them and placed his forefinger on the gold that rimmed the sapphire. "It is! It is! The very one the Master received on the night of his farewell performance!"

He stared at Auguste. "But you—how in this world of miracles did it come to you?" Complete astonishment arched his eyebrows.

Auguste appeared not to have seen or heard. He carefully replaced the medallion in its red velvet box, then enclosed it in the pouch. Last, he pinned it inside his shirt. He took four steps toward the door, passing Monsieur Bernard.

"Oh, no, I beg of you, don't go!" The teacher was now gripping Auguste's sleeve. "You see, he was my teacher, Hercule Hilaire, the greatest of us all."

Auguste was attentive, but his eyes expressed a resignation that might have been a hundred years old. He was as closed away as the hidden star of the medallion.

Monsieur Bernard's eyes glistened with tears. "I was notified of his death somewhere in the provinces but it was too late. He was honored by all Paris with ceremony, but that wasn't the same as seeing and talking with him just once more. But you?" He relaxed his grip on Auguste's sleeve. "Were you his pupil in his last days? Is it his magic I saw in you when you became the cat?" His tones were round with wonder.

Auguste stepped back. He slowly seemed to grow taller, to elongate. Even his face became leaner, older. His stance was that of a very old man. He mimed a small box in his hand, opened the imaginary lid, drew out something that by his reverence for it became precious. With an expression of utter tenderness he handed it to his own mirror image. The image accepted the object, the old man dissolved and Auguste returned to himself.

The tears now spilling from his eyes, Monsieur Bernard seized Auguste's arms and kissed him on both cheeks. "Then you are truly his inheritor, the Master's last apprentice. How he must have loved you to give you the star medallion!"

He then went to the window to blow his nose and wipe the tears from his face. "Perhaps," he said, his voice now very low, "perhaps he sent you to me. I don't know how, but the mysteries require no answers. They must simply be accepted."

He suddenly clapped the sides of his head with both hands. "But what by the devil's horns are we going to do about Madame Trollant? Her threat to withdraw her endowment is as real as an iron horseshoe. She wants you gone. She demands it. But wait!" His voice gained in force and determination. "That woman's power extends to the school but no further. She cannot interfere in my domestic arrangements. It must be clear, even to her, that this is my home as well as my place of business. You will remain, not as a student but as Madame Louva's assistant, and confine your activities during school hours to the attic and the kitchen and refrain from contact with the pupils."

Auguste looked at the master with an air of doubtful hope.

"That is an arrangement not likely to please Madame,

but we shall deal with the consequences as best we can. Are you ready?"

The resignation was gone from Auguste's eyes. Instead they seemed colored by light.

"We will begin now," said the master.

16

The next morning Auguste set off for the market instead of the first class. He was under Madame Louva's strict instructions to be aware of bargains but not to be fooled by low prices if the vegetables were limp.

He carried the list in front of him, knowing this would be a test of his capabilities. But before starting this new task he detoured two streets and arrived at Astair's cellar entrance, hoping to find her recovered.

The door was unlatched and he stepped into a sickness deeper than he had ever seen. The familiar dankness of the room now smelled of vomit. The girl, one leg over the side of her bed, was uncovered, the dirty quilt flung onto the floor, and she was muttering sounds that were not whole words.

Auguste pressed his palm over her forehead. Her skin felt like fire. She opened her eyes to the coolness of his hand and, though he couldn't be certain, she seemed to recognize him.

Auguste knew he must hurry to accomplish his duties and then inform Madame Louva. He ran all the way to the market, purchased what was needed, precise and swift in his choices. Just before leaving the crowded square he bought a bottle of milk. But a few minutes later, trying to urge the sick girl to drink it, he realized she was beyond him, out of reach in delirium.

Taking up the market baskets again, he was soon back in Madame Louva's kitchen. He placed them on one of the counters and then, pulling at her right arm, he pointed toward the street.

She began to check off the items as she took them from the baskets. "Do let off tugging at me, child. I've enough to do without further nuisances." She clucked admonishingly. "You forgot something. The potatoes. You'll have to go back."

He nodded, his face expressing such urgency the housekeeper's attention was finally focused on him. He indicated with the sweep of his arms the form of a bed, then sculpted the shape of someone lying on it.

"I cannot catch your meaning, *mon petit.*" Her concern for his evident distress marked her face with a frown. "But here, take this pencil and write it for me." She handed him the stub she had been using and laid out the back of the grocery list.

Auguste began to write, slowly, like a person much younger who had not been long in school. "Astair is very ill."

It took him so many minutes, Madame Louva's impatience seized the pencil from him and, placing a hand on each of his shoulders, she spoke directly at him. "You're begging me to come, aren't you? Like a little puppy. Well, just wait until I brown the meat for lunch and put it to simmer. Then I'll go with you, though I am already calling myself a fool-hearted old woman."

Auguste busied himself putting away the packages in the cupboards, the cabbage and onions in the bins, and finally he watched the housekeeper go into the hall, put on her large silk black hat with its three small roses tacked onto the front, and secure it with a long hatpin.

"Well, child, lead on. Where does this friend of yours live?" She continued to chat as they went down the street. "I must say I disapproved of her temerity—breaking into my house the day it was empty."

Auguste gestured a protest.

"Oh, I know you invited them in, but I've my own notion as to who thought it up. Monsieur Bernard didn't tell me why he is keeping you on after what happened to poor Raymond, but I'm pleased because I need help in the house."

She looked closely at the tall boy beside her, accommodating his stride to her shorter and slower steps, and with a very quick motion of her hand she impulsively swept the hair off his forehead. Then, gruffly, she said, "Are we to cross half of Paris?"

At that moment Auguste reached the cellar steps. He pulled her down into the dim room.

"By the Blessed Mother! What a pigsty!" she cried, then went straight to the restless figure on the bed. "This damp is enough to bring on the grippe and that's what the child has." She felt her face. "A very high fever." She lifted Astair to a sitting position. "Come, Auguste, don't stand there like a post. Help me wrap this excuse of a coverlet around her. We've got to get her to the house and call a doctor. I'm not one for charity outside my own family but this is too much."

They managed to prop the girl upright and half carrying, half dragging her between them, they finally arrived back at the school. Upstairs in the housekeeper's room, they laid her on the single bed.

Madame Louva was short of breath and her cheeks were as scarlet as Astair's. "There is a cot in the attic behind some packing cases," she told Auguste. "Bring it down while I get out clean sheets and a warm comforter. Hop to it!"

In ten minutes Astair was sleeping, her delirium quieted, as though somehow she sensed she was being cared for.

The housekeeper once more addressed Auguste. "Now I want you to listen to me carefully," she said. "There are going to be objections, a whole storm of them, from Madame Trollant if she discovers this sick child is here. So I shall say she is a parentless cousin from Anjou, arrived sick and needing me. Now go and fetch our neighborhood physician. 12 rue d'Entraigues. Hurry!"

ᕲ 17 ᕩ

Madame Trollant and Philippe, with Monsieur Bernard trailing, entered the house just as the doctor was leaving. Philippe's mother held to her face a handkerchief that had not been dampened during their visit to Raymond's bedside, as he lay partially conscious, both legs in casts. She did not miss the significance of the stranger's black bag.

A few minutes later, as she was graciously accepting an aperitif in the kitchen, she commenced her questioning. "And who is sick in this house?" she asked Madame Louva, who was busy wringing out cloths in a basin of cold water. "My son mustn't be exposed."

"Not Auguste?" said Monsieur Bernard, frowning.

Madame Trollant was diverted from her inquisition. "Do you mean to tell me," she said with dangerous calm, "that young criminal is still on the premises? I find it hard to believe that my demands have not been taken more seriously. Bernard, what do you have to say?"

"Indeed, madame," he replied, "you have my assurance that Auguste no longer attends classes and is forbidden social contact with my students. That, if I am not mistaken, is where my obligation to you lies. The boy works as an assistant to Madame Louva in my personal household where he is much needed and is expected to carry out such tasks for me as I see fit."

Madame Trollant sniffed. "You place yourself in a precarious position, monsieur, one I fear may prove disastrous to you. Despite the decision of the Sûreté to declare poor Raymond's injuries the result of an accident, I am more than inclined to believe you are harboring the malicious culprit. I have seen the unfortunate victim in the hospital, both legs in casts and barely conscious. It's a miracle he survived."

Monsieur Bernard inclined his head with the utmost gravity. "I take it he has not named Auguste as his attacker?"

"No, he has not. He claims to have fallen, a claim which may well be founded in fear of reprisal."

Philippe's grin was hidden behind a raised hand and a cough.

"In the meantime," said Monsieur Bernard, "Auguste's behavior will be watched for signs of viciousness and he will continue his employment. Madame Louva isn't getting any younger—like the rest of us."

Madame Trollant fluffed the tips of her hair. "Well, at least I don't have to concern myself with that." Her voice lowered to hardness. "But the doctor? I've not been answered."

The housekeeper dumped the water from her basin in a loud splash.

"Yes," said Monsieur Bernard, "who is this patient of yours?"

Madame Louva spoke directly to her patron. "She's a young cousin of mine from Anjou, come to Paris to work in a shop. But she arrived in ill health. So, with your permission, monsieur, I feel in all conscience I should keep her until she is able to resume her plans."

"Certainly," responded Monsieur Bernard. "With your care she will soon be well."

Madame Trollant shrugged. "Just be certain also," she said, "to keep her confined and away from my boy. It is only two weeks until the performance."

Monsieur Bernard's gasp was loud. "But it is scheduled for a month from now, just before the holidays!" he exclaimed.

"I've changed my mind. I intend to take Philippe to London for the Christmas season. We've a very important invitation for that period." She put down her glass. "So adjust yourself to the change, and if you are not prepared, adjust quickly."

She flounced from the room, then wheeled to face them from the threshold. "I am sure my son is thoroughly prepared. Come, Philippe!"

He followed her into the hall and out the front door.

When it had closed, Monsieur Bernard threw his hands upward. "*Mon Dieu*, what a woman! This means I must book the theatre for rehearsals immediately. Madame Louva, please telephone Monsieur Bragge this very instant and say I'm on my way to meet him. Thank God the students aren't coming today. Give my regards to your young cousin. I'll greet her later."

He rushed out before the housekeeper could caution him to wear his wool scarf.

Auguste came in from the corridor and Madame Louva did not require a clue as to what he wanted. "Her fever will go down as soon as the doctor's medicine takes effect. But she needs nourishment. I'm heating up some of my good soup, and you take it up to her. Get her to eat it even if you have to spoon it into her mouth yourself. You are friends. She'll do it for you."

Auguste nodded. The housekeeper turned to the stove, her back to the boy. For a few seconds he stood very close to the occupied woman and, without touching her, he encircled her with both arms. Then his arms dropped.

She looked back at him. "How odd," she said. "It was almost as though someone hugged me." She laughed at herself. "Embraces are few and far between for me these days. *Quel dommage*, eh? What a pity!"

Auguste was smiling.

"You know, *mon petit*, you may one day be handsome. You've the bones for it, just have to put on a few layers of padding."

She handed him a tray containing a bowl of soup and an ironed cloth napkin. "For her supper we'll add a piece or two of grilled bread. Now go, she may be hungry."

Auguste tapped gently on the door to the housekeeper's room. A voice less loud than a sparrow's said, "Come in." When he stood inside he smiled at the contrast between Astair's ugly cellar and this coziness. Furnished like a living room, the chairs were covered with red plush, the table and the mantel surfaces lined with family photographs. Astair's face, relaxed and clean, glowed against the starched whiteness of sheets and pillowcases.

He drew up a chair to the side of the bed and, tray on his lap, he waited for her greeting.

It came quickly. Her eyes, no longer blurred by fever, spoke for her. She said, weakly but with her old gaiety, "*Mon chevalier*, my knight." She hoisted herself higher onto the pillows. "Never thought I'd know one, but I do now."

Auguste dipped the spoon into the soup.

"I can manage for myself," she said and, propped on one elbow, she slowly began to eat, gazing around the room between swallows. "Look, Auguste, at all the people!" Then she pointed to a mottled blue vase choked with artificial tulips. "Wish I could get her some fresh ones."

Auguste mimed Astair's street singing and the girl laughed. "Yes, I'll earn them for her."

Auguste took a new pose, his head to one side as though he were listening to someone performing. He had become an audience.

Astair understood. "I have a song I've never sung before. It goes like this."

Let the day come soon
Let the day come bright,
I discard the moon.
For the game of night
Is a losing game
And a loss of sight.

Give me tomorrow,
One more time
To cancel my sorrow,
To pantomime
What might have been
With a silent rhyme.

Then I will leap
The fence of night
With nothing to keep
Me from the light,
And I'll be free
When the day comes bright.

The song ended, she spoke again, her voice diminished. "Will she let me stay until I am well? After all this, it will be difficult to go back to my own room."

She saw that Auguste was answering her worry with the reassurance of a definite smile and her lightness returned. "Reminds me of my grandmother's room in the country," she said, then gleefully added, "Never had a grandmother. You must learn when I am pretending and when I am not. But what are you doing here so long? I thought you had classes."

Auguste drew a high X across his chest.

"You mean you've been dismissed? But why? What happened?"

He got up and, hopping a line in front of her, momentarily became eight different people; he then ushered them all out and was himself, alone, doing exercises.

"I understand," said Astair. "You're working by yourself."

He took on the movements that were characteristic of Monsieur Bernard and he shook his finger at the now absent Auguste.

Astair's eyebrows raised. "He is giving you private lessons—the master himself? Oh, Auguste, you must be very talented or he wouldn't bother with you!"

Auguste crumpled into the stooped form of a monkey, scratching his head, and Astair flopped back on her pillows in laughter.

A few minutes later she fell into sleep. Auguste smiled, knowing she had accepted this temporary shelter.

❧ 18 ❧

The next week ran quietly. Astair recovered and her company was welcome to Auguste. Though still weak, she was able to help with his cleaning chores and on this Saturday morning, to accompany him to the market.

On their return journey, Astair carrying the lightest of the four filled baskets, she was suddenly overwhelmed by the shouts and back-clappings of her three street friends.

"What good chance to find you!" cried Jerome, his grin wide with delight.

"Thomas thought you had died," said Francois.

"Oh, cut that kind of talk!" commanded Jerome. "She's back and that's all that counts."

A brief scuffle closed the subject.

"But tell us—where have you been? We checked every day where you live."

She recounted with pleasure how Auguste had rescued her, the unfamiliar caring and comfort given by Madame Louva.

"And what do you have to eat?" they asked in chorus.

Astair smiled at Auguste. "We'll be late, won't we, if I tell them everything? I got you into trouble once and that's enough." She turned to the group. "Follow me," she called.

They fell in behind her and chanted in unison the song *"Le brave soldat"* that Astair had taught them long ago. Auguste pretended to be carrying the colors of the regiment, and he waved his flag to and fro with conviction and pride, the market baskets hooked over his arms.

When they reached the steps of the École Bernard, the little army dissolved, and they stood exchanging the latest street gossip.

Suddenly a voice silenced them. It was Philippe. "Get off and out of here!" he ordered. He was standing on the top step and did not stir from his superior position.

Astair spoke before any action could kindle a fight. "Remember—we make no more trouble for Auguste. He is one of us."

Her words held them but there was no mistaking then hostility toward Philippe. He was now an enemy and no to be forgotten.

When the boys had gone, Philippe said, this time to Auguste, "The master wants you in the studio, but remember you're nothing but a servant so keep to your place." He ignored Astair completely, and as the two boys hurried upstairs she went into the kitchen to help Madame Louva unload the baskets.

Monsieur Bernard was talking to the class. He nodded at Philippe and Auguste and indicated that Auguste was to sit at the back of the room under the window. He handed him a notebook.

"We have very little time to work up the performance,"

he began. "It will be difficult to memorize the exact details of the choreography. Auguste will record your entrance cues in order that he may assist me as prompter. From you I will expect double application and cooperation. Also, I have changed the last half of the play. In fact," he smiled, "I have complicated it. So listen well.

"You all know that the princess is enslaved by a demon. We never see this creature except as darkness. He has taken her into a forest of black-trunked trees with muted, multicolored leaves. The ground exudes fog and a terrible stench which for the sake of the audience must be imagined."

There was a little lift of laughter from the ensemble.

"Her lover follows them. The creature of darkness has set certain obstacles in his way: the first being a hedge of thorns; the second, a river he nearly drowns in; then scores of lighted, flying things burn him. He struggles through and finally arrives as the princess is about to be swallowed up in the creature's darkness. All these obstacles will be worked out with lighting. The hero fights with dwindling strength, and as his sword slices valiantly through the unseen terror, light begins to increase until it is fully returned. The creature is vanquished. That, in essence, is the action. Now I wish to rehearse the solos."

It was past noon when Madame Louva sent Astair to the studio to call the troupe to lunch.

The master dismissed his pupils but told them that he and Auguste would be a little delayed.

When they were alone, Monsieur Bernard put one hand on the boy's shoulder and spoke low and intensely but Astair, waiting for Auguste outside the door, could hear clearly.

111

"You are to follow the instructions I gave to you in front of the class. In addition to that, I want you to attend most assiduously to the choreography. Memorize it." He was now all teacher with no touch of affection. "In particular you are to concentrate on every aspect of Philippe's role until it is part of you. But—and this is most important for you to grasp—there is no hope that you will set foot on the stage. You will be working solely for the experience of learning. So no dreaming. Do you understand me? One more word—this must remain between us."

Auguste nodded his assent.

"I will now go down to lunch."

Auguste bowed and admired the princely dignity of Monsieur Bernard's departure with a few seconds of unconscious imitation. Would he ever achieve that bearing?

His revery was cracked by a pinch on his cheek. Astair signaled to him to follow her, and the two raced noiselessly down the stairs and into the kitchen, where Madame Louva was pouring potato soup into many bowls.

"Skylarking is not at this moment appropriate," was her only comment, and the two carried the first serving into the dining room.

When the main dishes had been placed before Madame Louva, both Astair and Auguste slipped into their seats, one on each side of her, and listened to the exchange of talk among the students.

Monsieur Bernard said nothing, seemingly bemused by his own thoughts, until the meal was over. Then he rapped his empty wine glass with a knife and said, "You have forty-five minutes to reassemble at the theatre." He got to his feet and left the room, the others close behind him.

Auguste hastily helped take out the dishes, then ran into the street.

Astair smiled at the housekeeper, the two of them stacking the plates in the sink. "Couldn't wait to get to the theatre, could he?" she said.

"Poor boy," murmured Madame Louva. "He'll never receive his chance in this life. Perhaps the next."

"But Monsieur Bernard is coaching him, is he not?" asked Astair, surprised.

"From that I fear will come only disappointment. As long as Madame Trollant is in control here the boy will not have a prayer of realizing his talent."

"But he's the most gifted of all! I know. Every day I see it."

Madame Louva glanced piercingly at the girl. "For a Paris gamine you are very naive. Why do you suppose Philippe is given the leads in all the shows? Oh, he's skillful enough to get by and learns quickly but—" She threw up her hands as if to say the truth was evident enough without explanation.

For the next twenty minutes, until the washing and drying were accomplished, the two were companionably silent.

Madame Louva then took out her large straw sewing basket, lidded with pink calico, and began to darn the first of a pile of socks. She gestured to Astair to also seat herself at the table, but an unusual awkwardness seemed to have taken the girl. She stood across from the housekeeper. Twice she opened her mouth and then closed it. Madame Louva waited.

Finally, in a voice quite lacking her usual vitality, Astair said, "I've never wanted to thank anyone for anything before, madame, but now"—she faltered, all confidence gone—"now I must."

"Not necessary, child. You were sick. You needed my help. I gave it, that is all. I would do the same for Auguste's cat." There was no trace of harshness in her tones.

"No," said Astair more strongly, "you don't understand. I am different than before. I think from the time I first met Auguste. I think"—her hesitation was brief—"I think I care more.'

Madame Louva looked up from her sewing. "That is indeed a good advance and I'm pleased. The boy isn't like the rest of us, is he?"

"No," said Astair, "and sometimes I hear more in his silences than in all the voices on the streets." She broke off and seemed to drop into remembering.

Madame Louva nodded, smiling. "You need each other."

The girl shook her head. "I might need him, but he— well, he is like someone who walks ahead of me." She laughed. "Never knew I had so much poetry in me."

She rounded the table and stood close to the housekeeper. She held out her hand. "Good-bye, madame."

"Good-bye? No purpose in that, child."

"Yes. I am myself again and must guard my independence. Don't worry. I'll come back often and will continue to be the porter of the market baskets." She released Madame Louva's hand, and before she could be detained was out and down the front steps.

The housekeeper settled back in her chair. "Peculiar child," she said to no one, then smiled. "I shall have to caution myself against becoming a sentimental old crone. That would never do at all."

﹌ 19 ﹍

Auguste went immediately to the theatre. The students had dispersed in other directions, and he walked alone onto the empty stage. It was lit only by the overhanging work-light; but he felt alive there, breathing the smells of dust, of wood, of old paint and, most pungent of all, the passage of humans. Two stagehands high above him were discussing the price of cheese as they adjusted the ropes attached to the backdrops. The whanging of a hammer came faintly from the rear of the theatre. A cleaning woman, vacuuming the boxes, was humming an old music-hall tune.

Auguste moved into the forest of painted trees and, losing all awareness of the present, he pretended he was still ten years old, practicing his master's exercises in front of a strip of sheet metal for lack of a mirror. At any moment Monsieur Hilaire would come up behind him.

When a hand touched his back he turned, half imagined his reverie to be real. It was Monsieur Bernard.

"This is the very same stage where Hercule performed,

where he received the medallion you now possess." The teacher paused to read the boy's eyes. "But somehow you knew this. His presence is here."

Just then someone summoned Monsieur Bernard to the back of the house.

Philippe's voice broke in. "It is really too much having that boy around every minute. I just can't swallow the excuse that's been given to us for his being here or the preference Monsieur Bernard shows for him. My mother will really raise a storm if I tell her."

Monsieur Bragge stood beside him. "Then keep it to yourself, please. If she withdraws her support now, I'll have an empty theatre for a month and that I can't afford. As to the dummy, Bernard insists he is necessary to his housekeeper and to him, so I'd shut up if I were you."

"Maybe for now," Philippe muttered.

Jean-Louis sidled up to his comrade as Bragge moved gratefully away. "I guess you know," he said, "that the girl Madame Louva took care of was off the streets. No more a cousin from Anjou than I am."

Philippe smiled tightly. "Perhaps that fact will come in handy. Auguste's friend, isn't she?"

"I know something else," continued Jean-Louis slyly. "I know what you've got against Auguste."

"Do you? Well, spit it out."

"None of my business, really." Jean-Louis was purposely offhand.

"Maybe not yours but mine!" Philippe seized Jean-Louis's wrist and squeezed. "Say it!"

"It's only a guess," the other boy ground out between clenched teeth, wishing he had never spoken.

"Then guess again!" ordered Philippe, once more digging his fingers into Jean-Louis's flesh.

116

"Let me go and I'll tell you. Auguste saw you push Raymond off the roof. Didn't he?"

Philippe let go. "Is that all? Well, the dummy can't tell, can he? And anyway, he won't. I fixed that. Go get my felt slippers from the greenroom and hurry."

Jean-Louis ran to obey.

He had only just returned when Monsieur Bernard called the cast onstage. "We'll do the first and second trials against the demon. Take it from where the youth's followers tell him farewell, just before he starts out to find the captor of the princess. Places!"

They began the stir of embraces, sorrow and the miming of farewell to Philippe. Then he began the long journey, running in place, advancing only a few inches for many strides. He came to an abrupt halt, throwing his body against an invisible obstruction. It was high and impenetrable.

Monsieur Bernard broke in. "No, Philippe, you're not telling me that the thing in front of you is studded with thorns, that the palms of your hands have been torn by them. As you know, we will have lighting effects to represent the hedge itself, but there won't be anything more solid before you than there is now. I want the correct reactions. Start again."

The good-byes were repeated, the journey taken, the wall of thorns met.

"Better, but less than best. Again."

After the fourth try Monsieur Bernard went onstage to talk to the group. Philippe stood apart from the others, scuffing his toe petulantly on the soft boards of the stage, until the master once more called for a repetition.

An hour later Monsieur Bernard announced a break. He was visibly tired.

Monsieur Bragge drew him aside and out of earshot of the troupe. "You should have gone through the river trial before this," he said. "It's just not working. Philippe is the problem, isn't he?"

Monsieur Bernard nodded. "I'm discouraged about him."

Bragge sighed. "He may not be good enough to be included in a history of mime, but he's not bad either and you know who pays the bills."

"You're right, as always, when it comes to practical matters."

Bragge's eyes suddenly widened. "I've got it! Why don't you show the boy yourself? Certain to be helpful, even if he simply imitates you."

"I've never liked to interfere with the performer's own interpretation."

Bragge shrugged and uttered one word, "Artists!"

But an hour beyond the break, after Philippe had inadequately demonstrated the struggle to swim the rapids of the fiend's river, Monsieur Bernard took Bragge's advice and climbed up from the front row onto the stage.

He ushered the troupe to one side with a single gesture and then stood tall and quiet, as if asking the attention not only of the men in the flies, the cleaning woman, his little audience of students, but of the bleak rows of seats, the dark stand of painted trees, the hollow orchestra pit, of even the great and unfilled space from stage to balcony.

Then, very slowly, he began to drown in the invisible river, to heave upward, his arms reaching for escape from the rapids, his head lifting for air.

In the wings, as still as the arch above him, Auguste held his breath, while the magic poured into his mind and body until he, too, was fighting the terrible rush of the river.

Monsieur Bernard stepped away from the illusion and back into himself, grayed and pale. There was a spontaneous burst of applause.

He bowed slightly, then turned to Philippe, his voice thinned by his efforts. "I do not want you to ape what I did. You must be your own feelings and movements. All I wished to show you was the innerness of the part. It must come from the center, your center, as it came from mine." He addressed the students, some still clapping. "We will break early today. Dismissed until tomorrow."

The group left together, pleased at the unexpected freedom.

When the last one had gone, Monsieur Bernard looked down at his hands. They were trembling. He walked into the wings, his expression pensive and closed. As he brushed by the side curtain he saw Auguste standing like a sentinel, and there was such joy on the boy's face the teacher paused to look upon it.

Then Auguste opened his arms wide like wings and lowered his head. Monsieur Bernard smiled in answer and his face was no longer gray.

～ 20 ～

Sunday emptied the school except for Auguste and Monsieur Bernard. Both Philippe and Jean-Louis had been called for by relatives, and Madame Louva was visiting a neighbor.

They had been rehearsing the play for an hour when Monsieur Bernard perched himself on the windowsill and called a halt. "Let us rest a while," he said.

When Auguste was seated cross-legged on the floor, he continued. "You may wonder why I seem to be training you into the part when there is no chance of your performing it." The words stopped and he seemed to drift into a kind of daydream, melting into the somber sky behind him that charcoaled the city.

He breathed deeply and began again. "I am sad this afternoon but perhaps"—he smiled in self-mockery—"perhaps it is merely the solemnity of the day outside. No. It started back when I was demonstrating to Philippe on the stage. I did what I had to do and did it well, but I knew my power was limited to only those few moments. They marked the extent of my stamina. Afterwards my mind brimmed with all the days and nights of my performing life and I woke up this morning knowing they were gone, as though they rested on the tips of my fingers and I blew them away."

He gestured the image. "But I believe that what gave me the most veritable sorrow was realizing that I had not advanced the tradition or even approached its pinnacle. I have served merely to keep it alive against a fading hope for its future. Then as I passed you in the wings and received your tribute of joy, I saw in you a hope of its continuing and going beyond what I had accomplished in my life."

For an instant Auguste covered his face with his hands, as if hiding from the master's words. Then he laid one hand over the man's foot, a contact both brief and light.

Monsieur Bernard could not summon a smile. "Yes, like that, like the children's game of tag. Now your turn has arrived. I cannot give you much but I can teach you what I know." He fell into silence.

Auguste gazed up at the master, who was now slumped, his eyes closed. The boy rose and from a moment of utter stillness moved very gravely into the paces of a courtly, ritual dance. He patterned out squares and triangles, often retracing the design.

The teacher was not fully attentive, but he felt himself move with the beauty of this formality, strict and certain as ancient music.

The dance ended and Auguste made a low reverence.

Monsieur Bernard leaped to his feet. "I am restored!" he cried. "You are all the applause I shall ever need!"

They went back to work, concentrating so hard they

121

didn't hear the soft footfalls on the stairs or notice the door opening to a crack as Philippe watched them.

He was down the stairs and on the telephone before a clock could tick. "Mother!" he shouted into the receiver. "Stop talking. Of course I'm all right! Listen, listen to me! Bernard is training the mute in my part! I saw him doing it! Come over right now!" He cut the connection with a slam.

Madame Louva, having overheard Philippe's call, did not show herself until the front doorbell rang. Then she went to let in Philippe's mother, who was so breathless with indignation her cheeks were the color of her peach blouse.

"Call Monsieur Bernard this very instant!" she commanded the housekeeper.

He was already on the first landing. He had no chance to give her even a *"Bonjour"* before she pounced.

"I thought you told me the mute was to remain only to assist Madame Louva!" she hissed.

Monsieur Bernard's face was impassive as he replied. "I am training him privately. This is my school and whom I choose to teach on my own time is my affair, no one else's."

"That may be true but that is only half of what my son has informed me. You are coaching this wastrel in Philippe's part. Justify that, if you please!"

"It may not have occurred to you, madame, but many hours of thought and energy are necessary to create the routines and variations of mime encompassed in Philippe's role. It is a simple expediency to make use of a stand-in so readily at hand." Monsieur Bernard was pleased to see the decreasing simmer of the woman's anger.

Madame Trollant turned to her son. "Perhaps you have made too much of this."

Philippe realized his partial defeat and, with an insincere apology to his teacher, he excused himself and went to find Jean-Louis.

He was in his room reading but tossed his book aside at Philippe's entrance. "What's the matter?" he asked. "You look as though you'd like to smash something."

"And I will if I have to," said Philippe enigmatically

"What? Who?"

"The dummy." Philippe's voice was nearly a whisper "I've a plan to frighten him off. Join me in my room after the household is settled for the night. *D'accord?*"

"Agreed."

After supper the housekeeper retired to her room, and Auguste was in his attic with his cat.

Philippe's instructions were concise. He and Jean-Louis were soon at Auguste's door. They flung it open.

Auguste was lying on his cot stroking the cat, who was spread over his stomach.

"What a tranquil scene!" Philippe sneered. He gave a sign to Jean-Louis who, as arranged, swiftly went to the bed and pinned Auguste down by his left arm. Philippe did the same on his right side. The cat jumped onto the floor and then to the window ledge. Its back arched and its ears flattened.

Auguste could not move.

"Now listen with both ears," Philippe growled at him, so close Auguste could feel his breath. "Be quite sure you hear me. I don't care what Bernard says about whom he teaches and whom he doesn't. You're learning my part and that I won't have. My mother believes Bernard. I don't."

He punched Auguste's chest. "If you don't stop your lessons, I make you a promise here and now that you'll regret it the rest of your life. Unless you do as I say, Jean-Louis and I will do a job on you that will leave you twisted as a crab. You'll be lucky to walk again—ever. I don't give a damn what excuse you give to Bernard as to why you've decided to quit. Just make it stick."

He motioned to Jean-Louis to release his hold, but before he too let go he wrenched Auguste's elbow. "Like this, only there'll be a crunch or two."

With a final swipe at the cat, which evaded the blow, Philippe and Jean-Louis left the room.

Auguste did not stir. His arms at his sides, he turned his palms upward and closed his eyes. Not even the cat's coming to lie in the angle of his shoulder persuaded him to open them.

⌐ 21 ↄ

The next day Auguste did not attend the morning classes, though he watched rehearsals at the theatre. Monsieur Bernard made no comment. Perhaps the boy wasn't well or was simply fatigued. But when Auguste failed to appear for lessons on the second day, his concern became anxiety.

He found Madame Louva in her room. "May I come in?" he said. "I must consult with you."

The housekeeper indicated that he was to take the armchair and then seated herself. Leaning slightly forward, her hands folded in her lap, she said, "It's Auguste, isn't it?"

"Yes. I don't know what has happened to the boy. Overnight he has become apathetic, unresponsive—even fearful."

"I have remarked it," said Madame Louva succinctly. She paused to underline her next statement. "We have to deal with a kind of twisted mentality."

"What are you saying?" exclaimed the teacher, almost

springing from his chair. "He is probably more normal than any of the privileged dilettantes who come to learn, and certainly more gifted. I'm shocked at what you say. I've always believed you to be a person of exceptional perception and feeling."

Madame Louva raised her hands, as if to stem this fountain of protest. "Please, monsieur, you misunderstand me! When your excitement is contained I will tell you what I mean."

Her patron, with some effort, sat down. "I beg you to do so."

"I was referring to Philippe and his follower, Jean-Louis. It is my belief that between the two of them they have contrived some sort of hold over the child."

Monsieur Bernard sat upright and gripped the arms of his chair. "Those two bullies," he said angrily. "I might have guessed them to be the source of the trouble. But tell me, madame, on what do you base your supposition?"

Madame Louva sighed. "Frankly, monsieur, I have no clue. It is not Auguste's poverty or muteness that has aroused Philippe's enmity. It is the boy's obvious talent. Young Monsieur Trollant's pretended disdain is but a poor disguise for jealousy, an emotion that produces the worst in the best of us."

Monsieur Bernard sank back a little. "Jealousy," he said. "Yes, Philippe has good grounds for that. If I were a young man aspiring to achieve a top place in my profession, I too might feel threatened by what I recognize in Auguste. Now, instead, I rejoice. It is like a miracle to find a link between the lost mastery of Hercule Hilaire and the future."

"But monsieur!" Madame Louva rose vigorously to the

defense of her employer. "It is you who have carried on his art. Don't imagine I haven't realized each day of all these years that I have been working for the greatest mime in France. You are the best in the world." She did not allow him to interrupt but continued. "You may imagine what you wish about the promise in that boy who knows next to nothing. I *know* what I know about you."

The angular lines of Monsieur Bernard's face softened into tenderness. "And who has kept me going?" he said. "Who has created a thousand repasts to strengthen me? Who has concerned herself with whether I was cold or warm and brushed the snow from my coat and dried out the rain from my shoes? Ill or well, who has cared this much for me?"

Madame Louva smoothed her already tidy hair and cleared her throat. "We are acting like two bad comedians. Let us return to our sheep, as my grandmother used to say when we wandered too far from the subject at hand."

Monsieur Bernard smiled and waited for her to continue.

"I am convinced," said the housekeeper, "that Philippe, alone or with his friend Jean-Louis, has threatened Auguste in some way. Otherwise he would never give up what you have offered him."

"Madame Louva, I am going to trust you with a secret, one I have only recently admitted to myself."

A knock on the door broke into his confidence. The housekeeper opened it to Astair.

"*Bonjour, madame. Bonjour, monsieur,*" she said smiling, certain of her welcome. She glanced around the room.

Madame Louva inspected her former patient. "You are wonderfully restored," she said, "and I am delighted to see you. *Ma petite,* if you will be so good as to wait for me in the kitchen I will be down directly and give you a cup of coffee. Monsieur Bernard and I are having a serious discussion."

"But of course." The girl stepped back and pulled the door closed. There she remained. She had heard the mention of a secret and would not miss knowing what it was. The voices came to her distinctly.

"What secret, monsieur?" asked the housekeeper.

"More than anything in my life I want Auguste to act the lead in the play. It is right for him and he is ready for it."

"But that is impossible!" cried the perturbed woman. "Madame Trollant would close the doors of this school tomorrow!"

"I know that," he said sadly. "Then what am I to do?"

Madame Louva's voice was of sufficient strength to penetrate a door twice the thickness of the one Astair was pressed against. "Nothing, monsieur, absolutely nothing! The final dress rehearsal is only two days off." She leaned close to him for emphasis. "I want a promise from you, monsieur, and you may think me forward for asking it, but I must."

"And that is?" said Monsieur Bernard gently.

"You will proceed exactly as planned. If you don't, it will be your ruin."

"I promise." The two words were almost inaudible.

Astair fled her post.

The housekeeper got up and unobtrusively let herself out. Her patron had fallen into a mood more sorrowful than she wished to witness.

When she reached the kitchen, the room was vacant.

She shrugged, mildly irritated. "Such odd impatience," she murmured aloud. "I would have sworn Astair was looking forward to a long, cozy chat."

⌒ 22 ⌒

The morning of the final dress rehearsal, the students went through exercises in the studio nervously. There was whispering behind Monsieur Bernard's back. He heard and ignored it, understanding the tension. Other students were pale and overly silent.

Madame Louva was washing the breakfast dishes, worried because Auguste had not appeared. She sent Jean-Louis to get him.

The boy, glad to evade at least a portion of the limbering up in the studio, lingered on the stairs as long as he could. Finally he tapped on Auguste's door.

He entered and found Auguste sitting on the windowsill staring out at the winter sky.

"Come on, dummy, the queen of the kitchen wants you," said Jean-Louis. When he received no response he was tempted to punch the still figure. Something—was it Auguste's deep withdrawal—held him off. Instead, he slammed the door behind him and took the stairs two at a time.

When Auguste heard him enter the studio, he got up

and went down to the kitchen. He stood, listless, beside the table.

"You're looking very dreary, *mon petit*," said Madame Louva. "I guess after all the hard work you've been doing for the master it's a real letdown to have your time free. Take your place and I'll pour you some coffee."

As she did so, she continued to talk, trying to lift him from lethargy. "Oh, I know what goes on here. I know, too, what the master thinks of you. And I know that is not enough for you." She lowered herself into the chair opposite him. "I was a singer once," she began in tones she might have used to calm a child. "Oh, not a headliner. I never made Paris, but the provinces knew me well. But the drafty dressing rooms and the snatched meals and the years added up and my voice diminished and my figure— well, that is obvious. Wrinkles webbed my pretty face— oh, yes, I was very pretty in my time—and I had to say adieu to all of it."

She saw that Auguste was listening, and the comprehension in his eyes was as old as if he had been a contemporary instead of someone a quarter of her years.

"But I have the good fortune to be Monsieur Bernard's assistant in life, for that is what I am. Yet when my mind begins to remember the bad with the good, the bad vanishes and what I have is not enough. So you see, child, I understand that young as you are, young and inexperienced, you are an artist and I know what you are feeling to be left out."

As though impelled by an invisible presence, Auguste rose. Pausing an instant in the doorway to look once more at the housekeeper, he went out into the street.

Madame Louva almost called to bring him back, but she sensed he wouldn't respond. When he didn't return for the noon dinner, her afternoon became increasingly worried.

Once the cat strolled into the kitchen and, for lack of a better listener, the housekeeper talked to it. "I wish I could send you to find him," she said. The cat meowed and then made its way to the back of the stove, where it curled up into sleep.

Monsieur Bernard had hurried off after lunch to the dress rehearsal with no time to discuss Auguste's disappearance. "I'll get supper near the theatre," he had told her.

Madame Louva scolded herself for her foolishness, but at five o'clock she put on her hat and coat and went directly to Astair's cellar. The girl was sewing a faded, plum-colored dress.

"What got into you yesterday? Why didn't you wait for me?" she demanded of the girl.

Astair ignored the questions. "I'll be wearing this to the theatre tomorrow night," she said, giving the housekeeper the one chair and perching herself on the cot. "I'm going with Auguste."

"Not unless we find him," said Madame Louva shortly.

"Why? Has he gone somewhere?"

"Gone is correct. Ever since this morning."

"What was the trouble?" asked Astair innocently. Astair knew everything. She was a listener at doors.

"That doesn't concern you, little one. The truth is, I'm terribly anxious."

"Go home, madame," said the girl, putting aside her sewing. "I'll alert my comrades. They're clever as rats at retrieving what is lost. Things or people, it makes no difference. You're tired, madame. I can see."

"Tired? I'm exhausted. But I've energy enough to want my child back in his attic."

"Your child, madame? He's yours?"

"Oh, no, not literally. Auguste is not mine or anyone else's and yet he is everyone's. But you are too young to understand."

Astair did not trouble the weary woman with a reply.

"Report to me soon," were Madame Louva's last words before she took her leave. "Good news or bad."

Astair thrust on her coat so hurriedly she widened a rip in her right elbow and ran outdoors. In ten minutes, she had gathered her three cohorts at the entrance to the cellar.

"You're to spread out, each taking certain sections. See? I've marked your routes on the sidewalk." She pointed to the lines scratched on the pavement, instructing each one.

They scattered speedily.

Astair had chosen the back alleys around the theatre as her territory and she was soon threading through this network of grimy, littered streets. Except for a few drunken men sprawled against the walls and cats touring garbage bins, she saw no one. The night wind had risen and it prowled the darkness, chilling Astair's hands white.

At last she gave up and entered the theatre, where the rehearsal was just ending. She waited until all the players and stagehands had been dismissed. Then she concealed herself in an unused dressing room.

She heard the doorman call *"Bonsoir"* to the watchman, who was having a cold supper in an upper office, and she came out of hiding. The work-light was the only illumination, hanging desolately over the forest set.

In the shadow of the open curtain she saw a wraithlike

figure walk across the stage and take its position in the center. She recognized Auguste—or was it he? His form seemed narrowed and, though he was completely still, there was a kind of pleading, a communication with someone who was not there.

Astair suddenly sensed that this unspoken conversation was over, and she ran out to her friend. "Come," she whispered to him. "I'll take you back."

He did not protest. Like someone blind and needing a guide, he allowed himself to be led out of the theatre and through the streets to the school.

Madame Louva was pacing the hall when Astair knocked. She flung open the door and after one glance at the boy, she put her arm around his waist. With Astair on his other side, they supported him up the stairs to the attic.

Removing only his jacket and shoes, Madame Louva bundled him tight in his blankets and kissed him on the forehead. "You must sleep now," she said. "There is always tomorrow."

He did not look at her but toward the window, where a shaft of moonlight shone brighter than his eyes.

↶ 23 ↷

Madame Trollant looked at her watch. "Seven-thirty. But where is my Philippe?" she asked Bragge as she paced Philippe's dressing room. "He knows what an important night this is for him."

Bragge was eager to be free of her to instruct the busy stagehands, the lighting crew and the ushers who were gossiping together like a flock of elderly crows as they untied the packets of programmes.

Bragge tried to reassure her. "He should be here soon."

"But Bernard called the cast for seven-thirty and now look. It's five minutes past the time. One can never count on anyone but oneself," she added petulantly.

"Be calm," offered Bragge. "He's with the others."

"No he isn't. He and Jean-Louis are having supper in a restaurant. He insisted. I should not have allowed it."

There was reason for Madame's concern. Astair and the three street boys had formed a blockade across the backstage alley. "You'll know Philippe when you see him," she said to her little army. "But we want them both, he and Jean-Louis."

135

"What if they come in a group?" asked Jerome.

"Then we cull them out, stupid." Astair's mouth was dry with near panic but she had to present a cool front. There was such an enormous chance of failure, not only with the kidnapping of Philippe but in the task of persuading Auguste to take his place. Maybe she couldn't do it. Then she remembered the lines of her song:

> *Que tu sois libre de peur*
> *Je te donne mon coeur.*
>
> That you be free of fear
> I give you my heart.

Somehow certainty sparked within her. It was fired by the sound of approaching footsteps. The boys suddenly lunged forward. Francois grappled with Philippe. Jerome attacked him from the rear and the two dragged their struggling victim around the corner of the theatre. Jean-Louis had darted a few feet toward the stage door when he was knocked down by Thomas.

"Where to?" asked Jerome.

"To my room, quickly! Keep them there until nine o'clock. Then release them."

The instant she saw them head for her cellar she raced to the school and began to climb the swaying steps of the fire escape to the roof.

It was now a quarter to eight and the first patrons were filing into their seats. The ushers were at their stations, their pockets full of small coins to make change for the confections they would be selling at the intermission. Conversations hummed in the high-ceilinged hall.

Behind the curtain there was no such order.

Monsieur Bernard had now joined Bragge and Philippe's mother in worry.

"I don't understand it!" he said for the fifth time. "My students, all of them, know the value of exact promptness. Your son and Jean-Louis are not exceptions."

"Certainly not!" said Madame Trollant, her indignation temporarily replacing near-hysteria. "My boy is exemplary in every respect." She relapsed into complaints. "My nerves won't take much more of this."

"Nor mine," muttered Monsieur Bragge, viewing the growing audience through a peephole in the curtain.

He was addressed by the stage manager. "Everything is ready, all standing by."

"Thank you," responded Bragge. "Tell the orchestra to fill in. We may have to cancel. The lead has vanished. I'll let you know."

Monsieur Bernard pulled out his watch. "It's only eight," he said with an optimism he didn't feel.

"Eight, nine, ten!" exploded Madame Trollant. "What do I care what time it is! My boy is missing. He may at this instant be lying dead in the snow, run over by a truck, shot by villains. Anything might have happened and you stand there worrying about the performance! I'm going to the police!"

"Give the boy another twenty minutes to get here," urged Bragge. "Then I'll do whatever you wish."

Monsieur Bragge stared at the stage door as though he could evoke Philippe's appearance simply by the intensity of his desire. He said hesitantly, "There is only one way to save the evening."

"And that is?" asked Madame Trollant, her tones so hostile she seemed to be spitting.

"Let Auguste take the part."

The woman let out a shriek that set their ears ringing. "This curtain will never go up without Philippe!" she shouted.

Meanwhile Astair had pounded at Monsieur Bernard's locked door. When there was no response, she crawled up the fire escape and along the gutters. She pounded on Auguste's attic skylight. "Let me in!" she called once, twice and then, even louder, a third time.

She was considering a way to break the glass when the skylight lifted. Auguste peered up at her with no surprise.

He held the window open while she scrambled over the ledge and down into his room.

"I have kidnapped Philippe. He will not be present to perform. I did it for you. I did it because you must become yourself, the true self that waits inside you, that has waited for this chance ever since you were born!"

Auguste only shook his head.

"No, Auguste! You must not refuse. Take it. I beg you to take it!"

He glanced at her once and then turned toward the window which was black with night and starless.

He would not do it for her. The attachment between them was not strong enough. Was there no way? She felt her heartbeat slow, her pulse weaken. She had to shock him somehow, to break this trance.

She spoke again, suddenly so angry she burned with it. Her voice was edged, knifelike. "How proud Hercule Hilaire, the great master, would be of you now! How proud to see you give up, throw away the gift he gave you!"

Her scorn cut at him. He flinched.

"Give me the medallion! You don't deserve to have it!"

Involuntarily he drew the pouch from his shirt and

handed it to her. Then, as though half aware of what he had done, he stretched out his hand to retrieve it. Astair had struck it from him, quick as a snake, and put it into her coat pocket.

He looked at her set and fiery face and he saw the challenge and the contempt. He reached for her hand, clasped it tight, and the two of them streaked down the stairs and out of the house.

As they rushed through the stage door the footlights were up, glowing on the great velvet curtain. Monsieur Bernard stood at its center, about to part it and step through to tell the audience that the performance had been canceled.

"Wait, monsieur!" Astair called to him. "He's here! Auguste is here!"

There was a blizzard of confusion. Auguste was costumed by half a dozen hands, all pulling and fitting and buttoning. The cast was alerted to the change. Monsieur Bragge quieted the impatience of the audience by announcing the substitution and instructed the musicians to continue playing. Madame Trollant, after simulating a faint, came around to enjoy a tantrum in the arms of two ushers.

At last the signal was given for the house lights to dim. The music quieted, ceased and began again as the curtain rose.

Monsieur Bernard nodded to himself in the wings as he watched his students mime the fairy tale. Auguste wove the part of the hero through the fabric of the story skillfully and without error in moving silence. But the brilliance his teacher had expected, had seen in the isolation of the studio, was missing.

Auguste was like an artist painting a tropic landscape

with only gray and brown. The colors, the vivid greens and scarlets, were missing.

As the curtain came down on the first half, the applause was generous, the atmosphere approving, but Monsieur Bernard was troubled. When Astair spoke to him he listened absently. She handed him the medallion saying, "You keep this for Auguste. He gave it to me."

"I wish," said Monsieur Bernard almost to himself, "I wish Hilaire were here. Perhaps then it would have happened." He put the medallion into his jacket pocket.

At ten o'clock the orchestra began the introductory music. Auguste stood ready for his entrance, just behind a flat painted as a tree. His concentration was so complete he neither saw nor heard the approach of Philippe, who had been released at nine as Astair had ordered. For several minutes he had lurked backstage, hidden.

Auguste felt himself seized around the waist. Arms pressed like giant pincers on his lungs. Then he felt a blow to his head as he wrestled his body around to face his enemy.

"I'm here to keep my promise. You remember, don't you?" Philippe slapped Auguste across the mouth. "I'm going to fix you so you'll never step on another stage, ever! Like this!" He smashed his right fist into Auguste's ribs.

Suddenly pain thundered through him. As though he had been thrust into another dimension, Auguste saw his own fists strike again and again at his tormentor. He was fighting for more than himself. He was battering at all the darkness of his life, too many shivering nights, the hunger, the savagery of those who had feared his silence. They rose in him like bile as he fought.

And then there was nothing to strike. Philippe had fallen.

Auguste was aware that Monsieur Bernard had him by the shoulders. "Can you go on?" he was asking. "Can you do it?"

He felt the hurting in his chest, his head and his left arm, but now he knew what he had to do.

He saw his cue and leaped forward onto the stage. He climbed the hedge of thorns, he swam the river, he penetrated the terrible, stinging swarm of needling insects, and last, he faced the creature of darkness.

The music from the pit was now a cello, a monotone of one note, the bow drawn harshly across the single string.

He drew out his sword and lunged at the invisible demon. He stumbled, he fell back and the stage darkened until only a faint glow spotlighted his wavering form.

The cello ceased and a silence as deep as death permeated the theatre. He fell to his knees, his face turned upward, seeing the full evil of what lived in this dark. He rose. He lifted his sword high above his head and the whole theatre seemed filled with a shout that had no sound.

With a final urgency, a last, triumphant attempt, he plunged the sword into the black heart of the invisible.

Then, very, very slowly, the spotlight brightened and grew wider and wider until it illuminated the entire stage.

The curtain came down.

Monsieur Bernard was the first to reach Auguste. He kissed him on both cheeks, leaving his own tears on the boy's face.

The applause and the yells of "Bravo!" reverberated so violently they shook the scenery.

"Go!" said the master. "Take the bows, the applause. It is yours." He gently pushed the boy through the parting of the curtain to take his first bow.

The crowd was now stamping on the floor, and when Auguste appeared the acclaim was pitched to wildness. Madame Louva was the first to stand, but five seconds later everyone had risen with her.

Four times, five, six, until at the seventh curtain call Monsieur Bernard knew Auguste could stand no more. He signaled for the cast to reassemble onstage and for the curtain to rise one last time. But just before it went up, he drew the medallion from his pocket and hung it around Auguste's neck. As he watched the boy walk out to accept what he had won, it seemed to him that the star shone with new light and that someone else stood beside Auguste in its radiance.

❧ 24 ❧

Very late that night, in Madame Louva's kitchen, they went over for the twentieth time, with laughter, Madame Trollant's scene in Auguste's dressing room after it had been cleared of the crowd.

"I thought she would burst like a melon!" chuckled the housekeeper. "And you, monsieur, when you told her you'd have no further need of her funds now that Auguste is with the company, you made me proud. She very nearly did burst."

"I saved one more arrow for my bow," said Monsieur Bernard, smiling broadly. "When Madame Trollant threatened to bring criminal charges against Auguste for assault, I informed her that Raymond has recovered both his health and sufficient courage to name Philippe as his assailant on the roof."

"I hope that young monster gets what's coming to him," said Madame Louva grimly.

Astair broke into delighted laughter and squeezed Auguste's hand. "No wonder she crept out like a chicken

143

without its feathers. She went dragging her little cockerel behind her."

Monsieur Bernard refilled their glasses from the champagne bottle on the table while Madame Louva retucked the blankets around Auguste's legs. Immediately on their return from the theatre she had insisted he be put to bed, but Auguste, still wearing the medallion, sometimes holding it in his hand, sometimes gazing down at it, had refused. So she had wrapped him up, only his arms free, in two thick blankets and allowed him the time it would take to toast their future.

"I was so proud!" said Astair, happily remembering how Auguste had rushed to her the moment the curtain came down. She almost told them how Philippe and Jean-Louis had been attacked and held. She thought better of it and said only, "A toast to friends."

"Your friends will be invited often to share our hospitality," said Madame Louva. "Is that not right, monsieur?" She had no doubt as to his reply.

"To be sure," assented the master, his smiles so quick and frequent they seemed all joined into one.

Glancing at Auguste, who was again dreamily looking into the core of the sapphire, Madame Louva rose. "Tilt up your glasses and drink to the bottom. Our new star must rest and, the good Lord knows, so must all of us." She leaned over Auguste and for the tenth time kissed his cheeks. He stepped from the blankets and threw both arms around her. For an instant he laid his head on her shoulder.

Her eyes filled with tears as she straightened him and, swiveling him about-face, started him toward the stairs. "March, *mon petit*!"

Auguste waved his good-nights to Monsieur Bernard and Astair, and as he moved up the stairs his steps quickened. When he came into the room, he went to the window as though he had been summoned and stood looking toward the stars, listening to the silent voice.

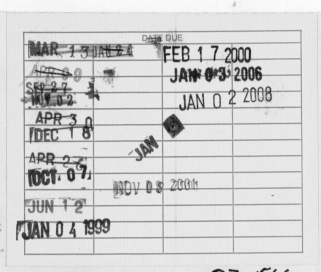